After Dinner Conversation Themes
Equality Ethics Edition
Philosophy | Ethics Short Story Fiction

After Dinner Conversation *Themes* – Equality Ethics

This magazine publishes fictional stories that explore ethical and philosophical questions in an informal manner. The purpose of these stories is to generate thoughtful discussion in an open and easily accessible manner.

Names, characters, businesses, organizations, places, events, and incidents are either the product of the author's imagination or are used fictitiously. Any resemblance to actual persons, living or dead, events, or locales is entirely coincidental. The magazine is published monthly in print and electronic format.

ISBN 979-8-9896194-5-0
Library of Congress Control Number: 2023952701

.

Editor in Chief: *Kolby Granville*
Edition Editor: *Kolby Granville*
Story Editor: *R.K.H. Ndong*
Copy Editor: *Spyrithon-Pyrro Rubanis & Kate Bocassi*
Cover Design: *Shawn Winchester*
Design, layout, and discussion questions by After Dinner Conversation.

https://www.afterdinnerconversation.com

After Dinner Conversation believes humanity is improved by ethics and morals grounded in philosophical truth and that philosophical truth is discovered through intentional reflection and respectful debate. In order to facilitate that process, we have created a growing series of short stories across genres, a monthly magazine, and two podcasts. These accessible examples of abstract ethical and philosophical ideas are intended to draw out deeper discussions with friends, family, and students.

Table Of Contents

* * *

From the Edition Editor

Most of our themed books have an edition editor, but those closest to my heart I have selfishly kept for myself. None is closer to my heart than this edition on equality ethics.

I did my best to select stories that covered a variety of equality types; realistically, we could have done an entire issue with just the LGBTQ stories we have published in the past. Instead I selected a variety of stories dealing with race, gender, sexual orientation, economics and economic opportunity, and ability, as well as housing status, among others.

I am in no way qualified to give deep insights into equality except the old cliché, when we know better, we should do better. And, of course, the accompanying idea, you can only open yourself up to knowing better by acknowledging there is always more to know. In my opinion, the person who "has it all figured out" both (1) doesn't have it all figured out and (2) is no longer capable of figuring out any more.

You see, I am of the opinion that morality is an infinite point and, once we stop talking and thinking about it, we have stopped walking closer.

That said, we should not chastise our former selves or others. Let's assume we were all just doing the best we know at the time. My greatest hope is that these stories will provide a tool for others to continue their journey. Dedicated to Casey Self, the first person to help me start my own walk.

Kolby Granville – Editor

A Wolf on The Bus

Matthew Wallace

* * *

Exhaustion flooded my body, leaving a dull ache pulsating just behind my eyes. With my right thumb and index finger, I squeezed the bridge of my nose, exhaling deeply, trying to soothe the pain. This tactic worked temporarily; at least until the bus hit a pothole or speed bump, sending jolts of electricity into my skull.

I reached into the yellow and red backpack that I had nestled beneath my seat and extracted a red pill bottle from the small front compartment. Twisting off the cap, I shook three oval tablets into my palm, threw them into my mouth, tilted my head back, and swallowed. I took another deep breath, allowing my body to relax as the medication entered my bloodstream. I could tell it was beginning to work when the bus hit one of the city's famous potholes, and I could no longer feel my brain jostling around in my head.

I stared out of the window that was centered directly across from me, watching the buildings and parked cars whip by. I always made a point to focus on the outside world when confined to a public metro bus. The seats faced one another, lined with your backs against the windows, and I hated the idea of potentially making awkward eye contact with a stranger.

Today, there was a woman sitting across from me. She held a baby that couldn't have been more than a few months old. I assumed it was her daughter due to the fact that she had it swaddled in a pink and purple princess blanket. The woman was looking down at her baby, and making popping noises with her mouth, which caused the little girl to giggle and reach for her mother's face. I couldn't help but think it was adorable, and felt a faint smile begin to curl around the corners of my mouth.

Distracted, I realized that I had been staring for a second too long, the mother glancing up and making eye contact with me. *Shit*, I thought, quickly averting my gaze further down the bus. I fixed my eyes on a man wearing a blue hoodie, scrolling through his phone and nodding along to whatever song his headphones were emitting. My heart leapt inside of my chest, and I could feel my cheeks getting warm with embarrassment, certain that they were now a light pink.

I was ready for this day to be over. Work had been an absolute nightmare, and to say I was tired would have been an understatement. My job as a clerk at the county courthouse was one that I took pride in, but the past few days had been overwhelming. Every day this week protesters had congregated in front of the building, chanting and waving their handwritten signs. To be honest, I wasn't all that sure what they were protesting; something about rights for all living beings. All I knew was that I couldn't step out of the building without being verbally assaulted, and that I spent all day getting yelled at by the courthouse's patrons, who had to walk through the crowd to get in the door.

"Shouldn't you be doing something about those Neanderthals," Mrs. Thornton, a 67-year-old crone living off of her deceased husband's social security, yelled at me.

"They're exercising their First Amendment right, Mrs. Thornton," I responded, along with a sigh, now used to hearing something along those lines from the people I was trying to help.

Mrs. Thornton huffed. "That's absurd," she snarled. "They should all be shot in my opinion. Good-for-nothings."

I can't say that I really agreed with people like Mrs. Thornton, but I must admit I felt annoyed at them for making my life difficult. People have the right to protest, and fight for their beliefs, whether others agree with them or not. That is what makes our country so great. I just wished they would pick a different place to do it.

My backpack began to lean against my left leg, indicating that the bus was beginning to slow as it arrived at the next stop. I glanced to the bus route map hanging next to the door, trying to decipher exactly which stop we were at. Following the red line that outlined the route, I could see that we were now at Bolivar Street, six stops before I would get off at Livingston.

I sighed, feeling as if I would never make it home.

The brakes on the bus squealed as it came to a complete halt, rocking me in my seat. The door opened, letting a warm breeze rush into the bus and compete against the chill of the air conditioning. My eyes remained on the bus route map, hoping to avoid any dreaded eye contact with the newcomers. However, periodically, and involuntarily, I couldn't help but glance over each person that stepped through the door.

First was a middle-aged Hispanic woman wearing light green scrubs, and a look of pure exhaustion consistent with that of a nurse just finishing a long shift. She walked between me and the mother holding her baby, taking a seat at the very back. I could feel her desire to be as far away from people as possible.

Next was a young man with round glasses wearing a Nirvana t-shirt, and a black backpack slinked over one shoulder. I suspected he was a college student either on his way to, or home from, class, as he sat down, pulled a physics book from his backpack, and began studying it intently.

Lastly, and unexpectedly, a wolf bound up the stairs and onto the bus. He was tall, but just short enough that he was able to step onto the bus with only his ears gently grazing the top of the doorframe. His fur was dark gray with white speckles surrounding his black snout, and he wore a blue Hawaiian shirt decorated with pink, white, and red flowers, along with khaki shorts and a pair of white Converse sneakers.

I felt my jaw slack and my eyes widen. Realizing that I was staring, I quickly looked around the bus, pretending I hadn't noticed him in the first place. In doing so, I could see that the other bus passengers were more shameless than I was, each of them with their eyes fixed on the wolf. The woman sitting across from me looked startled, squeezing her baby tightly against her chest.

The wolf, however, didn't seem to notice that he was the center of attention. He simply walked down the aisle and took the seat diagonal from me, next to the mother and her baby. The mother began to tremble nervously, and hastily gathered her things, moving down two seats from the wolf, but still stealing nervous glances at him. Again, he didn't seem to notice the behavior.

I myself felt slightly fearful, although I had never been personally attacked by a wolf or known anyone that had. There was just a certain stigma about them that most people couldn't get past. Wolves were bad news, and that's just the way things were. But even so, I couldn't help but feel bad for the guy. He hadn't done anything to anyone on this bus, and they were all looking at him like he could attack at any moment.

Once it was apparent that the wolf was the last one to get on the bus, the driver closed the doors, shifted gears, and pulled away from the curb. I glanced to the bus route map, confirming the number of stops left until Livingston Street: five to go. The air was full of an awkward tension that almost made it difficult to breathe. I reached and grabbed the knot in my necktie, pulling it loose and causing it to unravel. Balling the tie into a neat wad, I unzipped my backpack and stowed it inside.

My headache was completely gone now, but it had been replaced with an anxious itch in my temples. I studied the bus, making sure not to look at the same spot for more than a few seconds, and noticed that the other passengers were still staring at the wolf, seemingly afraid to take their eyes off of him.

I shifted my gaze to the wolf for the first time since he had sat down. He looked completely unbothered, scratching his chin with one of his paws. I observed his attire, curious why I felt the Hawaiian shirt made him seem less like a predator. I wondered if that were just a ploy he used to make himself seem approachable, and once you felt comfortable around him, that's when he would attack. Wolves were known to be devious, tactical even. Still, although stereotypes advised me otherwise, nothing about this creature seemed to be signaling any warning sirens in my head.

Wondering how he got his paws in his Converse, I realized that I had, once again, been staring for a second too long, the wolf looking in my direction and making eye contact. *Shit*, I thought, looking away as quickly as possible. I could feel his stare pressing against the side of my face, but I pretended that it had never happened, that I still hadn't even noticed he was there. A quiet huff, resembling a sigh, came from his direction, and from my peripherals I could tell that he had looked away.

The nudge of my backpack against my calf informed me that we were coming up to the next stop. A glance to the map; four more to go. The bus hissed as it was put into park, and the doors were opened, the warm breeze returning. The other passengers all stared at the wolf, hoping this was his stop, but the wolf remained in his seat, now licking his snout. He yawned, revealing his long, sharp pointed teeth.

From outside the bus, I could hear what sounded like muffled laughter. The sound grew louder and louder, becoming more distinct, until two men appeared in the bus's doorway. The first wore a black blazer over a white V-neck shirt with tight pants rolled up above his ankles. His hair was combed back, and a cross pendant dangled from his neck. The man's friend entered behind him wearing a purple and green striped, long sleeve crewneck, his pants styled the same as his companion's.

Once on the bus, the two men scanned the available seats. The man in the blazer noticed the wolf first, doing a double take and hitting his friend in the chest, pointing at him. Their cheerful demeanor died instantly, both adopting looks of disgust. I looked at the wolf, who was not paying them any attention. I felt an unexplainable twinge of pain in my stomach as I looked back to the men. They looked at each other, and nodded, before walking down the aisle, and taking seats on either side of the wolf; the man in the blazer sitting on his left side, crewneck sitting on his right.

The bus doors closed, and the vehicle lurched forward. The men stared at the wolf, but the wolf just continued to look forward, peacefully ignoring them. I felt bad for him, but at the same time was impressed at his ability to remain unbothered. The man in the blazer reached into his jacket pocket and pulled out a flask, unscrewing the top and taking a swig of its contents. He made a face that mimicked how he might look if he'd bitten into a lemon.

"Well, look here, Kevin," he said, passing the flask to his friend. "Looks like we found ourselves a lost puppy."

"Looks like it, Tristan. Maybe we should call animal control," Kevin laughed, accepting the flask and taking a swig. "Are there any kill shelters around here?"

The look in their eyes made me sick; smiles stretched from ear to ear, and a sadistic light radiating from their stares, like lions swarming for the kill. They were enjoying every second of harassing this wolf, which had done nothing to them, and I wanted nothing more than to stand up and punch them in the jaws.

"I don't know," Tristan said. "But I think he might look better as a rug in my living room. I'd hate for all that fur to go to waste at some kill shelter."

I looked around the bus, examining the other passengers. For the first time, none of them were paying attention to the wolf. They were each minding their own business: the guy in the blue hoodie was back to nodding along to music on his phone, the kid was reading his physics book, the nurse looked to be napping, and the mother was making popping noises for her daughter. Not one of them cared about what was happening right in front of them. I felt another twinge of pain, looking back at the wolf stationed between his two attackers.

"What makes you think you can ride the same bus as us?" Tristan jeered at the wolf. "You're an animal. Nothing more than a big dog. You don't deserve the same rights as us."

My cheeks began to burn with anger. I wanted the wolf to defend himself, to fight back. These men were disgusting and needed to be put in their place. I didn't understand how he could just sit there and take this abuse.

Do something, I thought, hoping he could feel me, *anything*.

Kevin laughed. "You think those protesters are going to help you with anything?" he said. "People will never see you the same as us. And they shouldn't. You're just a filthy beast."

Tristan furrowed his brow, frowning. "Hey," he yelled, slapping the wolf in the back of the head. "Are you deaf? He asked you a question." When the wolf didn't respond, he added a shove in the arm.

That was as much as I could take. What these men were doing was wrong, and someone, anyone, had to do something.

I stood, grabbing the handrail above my head, and pointed at them. "Stop it!" I yelled. "Leave him the hell alone! He didn't do anything to you!" Adrenaline coursed through my veins, anger swelling within me.

The two men looked at each other and started laughing. Kevin handed Tristan back his flask, and Tristan took a big swig before capping it and putting it back in his jacket.

He looked up at me and smiled. "And what're you going to do about it?"

I wasn't sure how to answer, but I knew I couldn't falter, or they would never take me seriously. I went with the first thing that came to mind. "I'll call the police," I said, trying to sound as authoritative as possible. "I'll report you for harassment."

Tristan narrowed his eyes, standing and grabbing the handrail above him. Kevin followed suit. They looked me up and down, sizing me up, then Tristan smirked, and said, "You're going to run and tattle on us? Go ahead. They won't arrest us over a wolf."

I feigned a smile, trying to look confident. "I work at the courthouse," I said. "I have a lot of friends in high places. I can make it happen, and make it happen quick."

Tristan took in my appearance: a navy suit, brown dress shoes, and a maroon button up indicated that I dressed the part of someone that worked in a courthouse.

I felt my weight begin to shift to the side as the bus began to slow, arriving at the next stop. The brakes squealed again, and I did my best to keep my footing while maintaining eye contact with my opponent, as the bus came to a complete halt and was parked.

We continued our stare off for a moment longer. Then, Tristan released his grip on the handrail, slapping Kevin on the chest, and saying, "Let's go. This is our stop." He stepped past me—shooting daggers from his eyes—looking away when he got to the stairs, and ambled off the bus, Kevin following close behind.

The other bus passengers all stared at me, each

redirecting their gaze when I locked eyes with them. I looked down at the wolf, who was looking back, appreciatively. Exhaling deeply, I reached down and grabbed my backpack, then took the seat next to the wolf.

"Are you okay?" I asked.

The wolf looked at me, but I avoided his gaze, looking at the seat I had just vacated. "Yes," he said. "I'm fine."

"I'm sorry about that," I said, softly.

"It's okay," the wolf said. "Unfortunately, it's something you get used to."

No one got on at this stop. The bus doors closed, and the driver pulled back onto the road. Three stops to go.

I cleared my throat, hoping this wasn't awkward. "My name is Joseph," I said. "Most people call me Joe."

"Nice to meet you, Joe," the wolf said. "I'm Remus. Most people call me Remy." There was a pause between us, neither sure what to say next. "Thank you," Remy finally said, "for what you did."

"It wasn't right, what those guys were saying," I responded. "I hope you know not all humans think that way." I looked at Remy for the first time and noticed that the corners of his mouth looked to be twisted upwards, smiling.

"A lot of society sees me as an animal," he said.

I felt bad for him, having to feel looked down on at all times. "Why wouldn't you stand up for yourself?" I asked, thinking about how he simply ignored the guys berating him. "You're a wolf. I'm sure you could've torn them to shreds if you'd wanted to." I smiled, hoping that would come off jokingly.

"I could have," Remy agreed. "But what would that prove? That would just make me look like what everyone already thinks

I am. People have an idea about wolves, and I have a responsibility to prove them wrong."

Listening to Remy, I found myself growing more and more respect for him. There was a big picture of peace and harmony between all living beings, and I realized now that this wolf was in a constant battle, every day, to try and achieve that goal; always having to look the other way, or be the bigger man—no matter how hard it was—all for the sake of something bigger than himself.

"You must not like humans very much," I said, feeling pity toward him. "They're so insensitive. I can't imagine being in your shoes."

Remy chuckled, which sounded more like a lawnmower with a loose blade. "On the contrary, I love humans," he said. "I have very good human friends. I have a lot of hope for humankind and I believe that change is possible."

"But how?" I asked. "When people can be so ugly and demeaning? When guys like that can say such hateful things to you?"

He looked at me, eyes full of light. "Because for every bigot like that," he said, nodding his head toward the door, indicating he was referring to the men that had exited the bus, "there's a human like you. Someone willing to stick up for what's right. Someone willing to fight and acknowledge when something's wrong." He paused, keeping eye contact and allowing me to feel the power of his words. "Yes, I could've done something to stop them, hurt them even," he continued, "but right or wrong the law will never side with a wolf. Unfortunately, that's just how society works right now. It will take people like you to make real change, because humans have to make other humans see the difference between right and wrong. Until that time comes, I just have to sit here and take the hate, and the anger, because I have to make that change a possibility."

I felt so small, guilty even, for living a life full of so much ignorance up until this point. My thoughts landed on the protesters outside of the courthouse. It was disheartening to recall the amount of ugly things that people, myself included, would say about them when they were just fighting for beings like Remy, trying to make a difference and make the world a better, more equal, place to live. I felt ashamed of myself for not taking the time to look outside of the small bubble that I lived in; ashamed that I wouldn't take just one second to put myself in another's shoes. In the short conversation we'd had, I could tell that Remy was more sincere and kind than most of the humans that I knew. Yet, he was treated as nothing more than an animal by most of society.

Through the windshield at the front of the bus, I could see the sign for the Lilac Street bus stop approaching. The bus driver eased onto the brakes, a high-pitch squeal emitting from the tires as a result. Once parked, the doors swung open and what sounded like the static crackle of a walkie talkie could be heard: a voice saying, "Yes. That's the bus."

"Got it. We're entering now," someone responded into the walkie talkie. "Over."

A police officer appeared in the doorway, his partner following close behind. The first officer was bald, wearing a pair of aviator sunglasses, and a name badge that read: Officer Lopez. His partner, trailing him up the stairs, had a red goatee and a high and tight haircut. His name badge read: Officer Keaton. They looked over the bus's passengers until they spotted Remy, then made their way up the aisle, stopping where we were seated.

The officers looked down at Remy with accusing eyes.

"Is everything okay, officers?" I asked, raising my eyebrows.

Neither of them looked at me, keeping their sights trained on Remy. "We received a call from a couple of gentlemen stating that there was a wolf on this bus causing some issues," said Officer Lopez.

"Threatening to eat everyone on the bus," added Officer Keaton. He reached behind his back and retrieved a pair of handcuffs from one of his belt compartments.

Officer Lopez beckoned with his hand like he was grabbing at the air. "Please stand up," he said to Remy. "We're going to need you to come with us."

I couldn't believe what was happening. Realizing who must be behind this, I felt my cheeks begin to burn with anger, wishing those guys had stayed on the bus so that I could yell at them some more. I opened my mouth to say something, but before I could, the mother holding her baby was on her feet next to me.

"Leave him alone," she said, still rocking her daughter. "He didn't do anything."

The officers looked at her, almost as shocked as I was. "Ma'am," said Officer Keaton, lifting his arm, signaling her to back away, "you need to stay out of this. You and your child don't need to be in the way if this wolf turns violent."

"He's not going to turn violent," she retorted. "He hasn't done anything to anyone."

"Yeah," came a voice from further down the bus. I turned

to see the guy in the blue hoodie now standing on his feet, one headphone dangling on his chest. "There were two guys on here earlier harassing him. They hit him and were calling him all sorts of slurs, threatening to kill him."

The other bus passengers, driver included, began to murmur in agreement, all standing up for Remy. The officers looked at each other, confused, unsure what to do or say.

"I believe there are plenty of witnesses here to corroborate what happened," I said, still baffled. "I also believe it's illegal to make a false police report, and there are other men you should be looking for." I hoped, from the bottom of my heart, that they could actually find those guys and give them what they deserved.

Officer Lopez leaned in and whispered something to Officer Keaton, who began nodding and put his handcuffs back into his belt compartment.

"Look," said Officer Lopez. "If all of these people are negating the report, we can't bring you in. But I would suggest that you get off at the next stop."

"That happens to be my stop anyways," Remy said, the corners of his mouth curling up.

The officers didn't say anything else, turning and exiting the bus. The driver shut the doors behind them and put the bus in drive. I looked around the bus, noting that each passenger had returned to their seats, and resumed what they had been doing like nothing had happened. Occasionally, one would steal a glance at Remy, but immediately look away.

Remy looked at me. "See," he said. "I told you."

"What do you mean?" I asked.

He let loose another chuckle. "When I first stepped on this

bus, everyone was afraid of me," he said. "I may ignore it, but I do notice the looks. And when those guys were harassing me, they pretended like nothing was happening." He took a deep breath. "But then you stood up for me. You showed them what was happening was wrong and they noticed. Then, when the time came again, they understood what needed to be done."

He was right. Twenty minutes ago, everyone on this bus was petrified of Remy. No one could take their eyes off of him, and then, once he needed help, they pretended he didn't exist.

"Humans have to make humans see the difference between right and wrong," he continued, repeating himself from earlier to proclaim his point. "It's the only way that we can make real change in this world, and I can't tell you how much I appreciate you for doing your part to help, Joe."

The bus came to a stop, parking at the Vaughn Street bus stop.

Remy stood. "Well, this is me," he said. "It was nice to meet you, Joe. Maybe our paths will cross again."

I stuck out my hand to shake. "I really hope so, Remy," I said. "You be safe." Remy extended his paw, and I wrapped my fingers around it, moving our arms up and down. When I let go, he turned and descended the steps, exiting the bus.

Relaxing my shoulders, I sank into my seat, exhaling heavily as the bus resumed its route. I felt pride for being able to help Remy; overjoyed that I, and the other bus passengers, had done the right thing. This world was in a tragic state, and it was deplorable that every being wasn't able to wake up with the same sense of safety and equality on a daily basis. I felt shame that I lived in a society filled with so much hate and violence directed at the less fortunate. We are all equal and deserve to be treated as such.

For the first time, however, I realized that perhaps I could be part of the solution. Perhaps I could go to the protests and sign the petitions and raise awareness. It's time for a change, and everyone has to step up and be there to help.

I looked around the bus, looking at each of my fellow passengers. Maybe Remy was right. Maybe we can change. My eyes landed on the bus route map. One more stop.

* * *

This story first appeared in the After Dinner Conversation—May 2021 issue.

Discussion Questions

1. The narrator admits he has never had a negative interaction with a wolf, so why was he initially concerned when a wolf stepped onto the bus? How do you think he got his initially negative opinion?

2. Is it right to be scared of someone that "looks scary" even though that particular individual may be perfectly fine? How do we learn what "looks scary" and are those sources reliable?

3. If you were in the position of the narrator, would you have stood up for the wolf? Have you ever stood up for a stranger in a real-life situation that was being abused or bullied? What causes some people to act, while others do nothing?

4. Do you agree with the wolf when he says his best strategy is not to fight back, but to hope that other humans will fight back on his behalf? Do you think the wolf should have defended himself?

5. To what degree do you think the lessons from the story are applicable to race relations today?

* * *

Teddy And Roosevelt

Steven Simoncic

* * *

They call it *Friends Group*. But there are no friends, and there is no group. Just me, a state-funded social worker, and another sixth-grader the kids call Sweaty Teddy. We sit in a converted cinderblock office between the furnace and the chapel and listen to the muffled sounds of the rest of the middle school having actual recess outside. On the desk, Ms. Judi has placed a stress ball, a *point-to-the-bad-touch* doll, a box of tissues, and a bowl of candy. She has been meeting with me individually every Monday for forty-five minutes of stress-inducing awkward silence since I transferred from Rosa Parks Elementary. Teddy is a Friends Group veteran. According to Tommy Stanick, my assigned locker partner, Teddy has been going to the *nut ward* since third grade when he threatened a teacher with an X-ACTO knife in art class.

Ms. Judi decided to put Teddy and me in a group session so we could dialogue. So far, I've learned that *dialoguing* usually just means Ms. Judi repeats the last thing I say in the form of a question.

"How are you feeling today, Roosevelt?"

"I dunno. Little anxious, I guess."

"So, you're feeling a little anxious?"

I nod. She writes something down. Teddy unwraps another piece of candy and pops it in his mouth. To escape his hard candy crunches, I do what I always do when I don't know what to do—I pick up my book and begin to read.

"The Strenuous Life," she says.

I nod.

"Still reading it," she says.

I nod.

"Can you read us something?"

I open the book to any page and close my eyes. "Far better it is to dare mighty things, to win glorious triumphs, even though checkered by failure, than to rank with those poor spirits who neither enjoy much nor suffer much, because they live in the gray twilight that knows neither victory nor defeat."

"That's impressive," she says.

"Teddy Roosevelt was an impressive man," I say.

"No, that you memorized that passage."

I nod.

Without looking up, Teddy slides one of the hard candies he has taken from the bowl over to me. I accept the gift. As I place the book back into my backpack, the edge of another brittle page flakes off and flutters to the floor. When the firemen left, they gave me and my mom anything of my dad's that they could salvage. His *fifteen-years-of-service* watch from Wayne State, a few teaching awards, his master's degree diploma, and his soggy, signed first edition of *The Strenuous Life*, which he read to me every night before bed—the book from which I can recite not one passage but any passage. And that is impressive. But I do not feel the need to tell Ms. Judi that.

"Teddy, why do you think you're here?"

This catches Teddy by surprise. He clears his throat, and for a brief second, the sour ball in his mouth goes down the wrong pipe. A series of coughs, snorts, and breathy exhales follow. He regains. His cheeks flushed red. His uniform shirt suddenly more sweat-soaked than usual, hopelessly untucked, and hovering above an ever-descending pair of khakis that no longer fit.

"I think we're here because I'm fat and he's Black."

We both look up from our laps at Ms. Judi. Waiting for her to say, *so you're saying you're fat and he's Black*? But instead, she opens up both of our files and begins to write.

* * *

The walk to school was always the same. I'd pass Michael Drostey and Ronnie Bootrie getting high on the corner of Westwood and Tireman. At Derby Hill, I'd see Gina and Tammy, two white girls who wanted to be Black, listening to Controversy. They shared a pair of foamy orange Walkman headphones, listening with wide eyes and shrieks of delight like they were getting away with something. And they were. Controversy was controversial in Copper Canyon—our little corner of Detroit that had no copper and no canyons. Just house after house of Detroit police officers who had to live in the city they pledged to serve and protect. So, they begrudgingly colluded to live in one neighborhood, a white island that shone like a new badge, with St. Agatha's at the center of their planned community.

I was not part of the plan. After the fire, my mom had to go back to work. She applied for a job in Mayor Coleman A. Young's office as an executive assistant to the Head of Human Services. The day of her interview, she was armed with an associate's degree from Wayne County Community and a ten-year-old resume. After I helped her pick out her clothes (three times) and put on her makeup (twice), I slipped a note in her purse to calm her nerves.

The credit belongs to the man who is actually in the arena, whose face is marred by the dust and sweat and blood – T. Roosevelt.

Except I changed the world *man* to *woman* and added a bunch of fireworks and flowers and hearts. I think it helped. She got the job. This meant we, too, had to live in the city. But we were done with Corktown, so we came to The Canyon to be safe.

I get to the top of Derby Hill, and by the graffiti-covered cannon, he is standing there. Teddy. We stand for a minute facing each other. I pull my inhaler out of my pocket and pump it twice. Teddy Roosevelt had asthma too. Mine acts up when I am near dust, mold, or confrontation. I'm not sure about Teddy Roosevelt's asthma. I have not been able to find adequate detail on his symptoms or triggers. Tommy Stanick passes by on his Mongoose. He flips me the bird. I don't know why.

"He's a dick," Teddy says.

I nod.

Teddy reaches into his backpack and tosses me a Sour Ball. I pop it in my mouth, put my inhaler back in my bag, and start to walk toward school. With Teddy.

* * *

Theodore Roosevelt began boxing at age fourteen when a *couple of bullies taunted and manhandled* him. I started at eleven.

He trained with the *Boston Strong Boy*, Jim Sullivan. I trained with my mom. He went from a sickly kid with asthma to fighting in the Harvard Gym Championship on March 22, 1879. I have asthma and have settled for trying to teach Sweaty Teddy how to punch. In the hours between school and dinner, Teddy and I were pretty much on our own. My mom worked until six or seven most nights, and Teddy's dad was a real gung-ho hoorah cop who was put on a special narcotics division in my old Corktown neighborhood. He was a gangbuster, *ballbuster*, Teddy would say. Total badass.

"It's a pillow," Teddy says.

"It's a punching bag."

"Made from a pillow. This is stupid."

"This will get them to stop calling you Sweaty Teddy."

I hold my homemade heavy bag. Teddy punches.

"That was terrible. You have to rotate. You punch with your hips, not your arms. Watch."

He holds the bag. I throw a combination.

"Damn! And you're so skinny."

"You think I hit hard? Teddy Roosevelt was—"

Teddy throws a left to my chest.

"Fuck! Teddy! Roosevelt!"

"Oh, it's on."

We wrestle to the ground, laughing, rolling on the burnt-out grass of my yard, throwing jabs, and talking shit until Teddy ends up sitting on me.

"Don't tell me—Teddy Roosevelt used to get sat on all the time."

"Fuck you, Teddy."

"Fuck you, Rosie."

* * *

On Saturdays, I visit my dad. St. Hedwig's Cemetery is exactly 9.4 miles from my house. My mom used to drive me every week, but that was before she started spending Saturdays with Phil. I usually take my bike, but Teddy popped my back tire bunny hopping a curb, and my mom won't let me take the bus ever since those kids got shot in Warrendale.

"Paul Ray has a car."

Teddy's half-brother not only drove but smoked and had a tattoo and a ring of hickeys on his neck. He spent most days ditching high school and practicing his nunchucks on *his corner*. Teddy was pretty much terrified of Paul Ray, but since I was teaching him to box, he felt like he owed me. I waited across the street, watching Teddy talk to Paul Ray. Through the slats of the wooden fence Big Ray built, I could see the brand new, four-foot-high, aboveground pool they just put in. The sunlight bounced and shimmered off the surface. A big green inflatable turtle floated dumbly back and forth across the pool.

I could see Teddy shifting his weight and not making eye contact. At one point, he popped a sour ball for moral support. As they talked, Paul Ray would line up Pepsi cans on the fence and crush them with his nunchucks. Each time Teddy would flinch and step slightly further away. The rumor in Copper Canyon was that Big Ray had to save Paul Ray more than a few times down at the precinct. There was talk of drugs. And fights. All Teddy would say is that Paul Ray would have been better off in jail than having to come home and deal with Big Ray. When Paul Ray broke his arm, everyone at school said Big Ray did it. I never asked Teddy about it. And he never told.

Teddy waves me over from across the street. I watch Paul

Ray watch me walk toward him, pretty sure I am not what he was expecting. I say thanks. He says nothing. Teddy shoots me the *shut-up* look, and we all pile into Paul Ray's burgundy Monte Carlo with crybaby rims and a petticoat spoiler.

The back seat is immense. Teddy and I bounce up and down as Paul Ray tries to scare and impress us, fishtailing down Warwick and laying a huge patch as he leaps off the line at a stop sign on Belton. Being a cop's kid in Copper Canyon meant you had license to do pretty much anything you wanted behind the wheel. And Paul Ray does. As we made a left on Telegraph, I tried to yell to the front seat that we were going the wrong way. But between Foreigner Four on the Alpine, and the growl of the *dirt mother* muffler he put on himself, Paul Ray didn't hear me. Or didn't care.

We pull up, not at St. Hedwig's, but at Sheri Olshenski's house. She was famous in Copper Canyon for almost getting pregnant. It seemed to happen a lot. Paul Ray lays on the horn. She comes out a minute later. Torn jean shorts. Cowboy boots. Teddy and I watch her walk down the driveway toward the car. She gets in, doesn't even look at the back seat, and begins to make out with Paul Ray. This goes on for a while. I try to whisper to Teddy that we should go, but he shushes me, eyes fixed on the front seat. A minute later, we hear the thuddy ca-chunk of the Monte Carlo's automatic doors unlock, and we slide out the passenger side.

The last mile of the walk was the worst. The hazy smokestack Detroit sky held the heat like a plastic bag. Soaked and slow, we walked toward the hill where my dad was laid to rest. I made the time go by faster for Teddy by summarizing my father's master's thesis: *Theodore Roosevelt: Politics, Patriotism, and*

Preparedness.

When we get to the grave, I reach into my bag and get to work.

"You always keep that in your bag?"

"Never know when I'm gonna get up here."

"It's like a tiny shovel."

"It's a trowel."

I clear the crabgrass and weeds off the headstone with my trowel. On my hands and knees, I blow the tiny blades and leaves out of the recesses of my father's name, birthdate and death date. Teddy watches. Gets down on his knees. And blows as well.

"We must show not merely in great crisis but in the everyday affairs of life," I say.

Teddy nods. Understanding the quote.

"And all men must try really hard in the arena of their life," he says.

I nod. Understanding he's trying.

* * *

As the weeks went by, we worked at being better at life. Teddy got better at boxing and doing his homework. I got better at being less judgy and more normal, and we both got better at answering Ms. Judi's questions. On the playground, we found corners and nooks to disappear into. Safe havens far from every Tommy Stanick, Ronnie Bootrie and Michael Drostey. We created our own world, and together, we preached and lived *not the doctrine of ignoble ease but the doctrine of the strenuous life*.

On our last hot dog lunch of the year, Teddy and I ate alone, together, like we always did. I gave him my second hot dog. He gave me half his sour cream and onion chips. After that, we were supposed to have final period recess, but since our homeroom earned enough *self-control marbles* in Mrs. Garko's Shush Jar, they let us out early.

My mom was working late. Big Ray was at a DPOA union meeting, and Paul Ray was getting hickeys from Sheri. So, we went to Teddy's house. It was the first time I was actually inside. Teddy's mom was away visiting her sister again. He said she had been gone for a while this time, but she called Teddy every Wednesday and Sunday to check in on him. Big Ray said Teddy was in charge of cleaning. This meant the house was never cleaned, but with Big Ray's work schedule and Paul Ray's Sheri schedule, no one was around much to care about the house. But the yard. The yard was perfect, with an Aqua Leader pool and a little wooden deck Big Ray built out of scrap from the privacy fence.

Teddy made us homemade Nesquik chocolate milk since my mom wouldn't let me have it at home. We sat on the deck. Our feet dangling in the water. Teddy found a cloud that looked like a snow cone with a human baby head. I found a buffalo.

"Why'd you do it?"

"Do what?"

"The X-ACTO knife."

The big green turtle floats toward us, gently bumping its face into my foot.

"They were calling me fat."

"They always do that."

"Exactly."

"So, you're saying, *exactly*?" I say in my best Ms. Judi voice.

Teddy smiles. Nods.

The snow-cone-baby-head cloud passes over us, blocking

out the sun. For a minute the traffic seems to stop, and we can hear the wind and the birds of Copper Canyon.

"I got so tired of being the fat kid. I just wanted to be something else. You ever feel that way?"

Teddy's looking at me now. He's almost always looking down. But now his eyes are wide. His face is open. A chocolate milk mustache beginning to dry and crumble around his lips. He looks innocent. Like maybe how he looked before any of this happened.

"We should swim," I say.

Teddy looks down again.

"No, I... I don't—"

"You don't swim?"

"I swim."

"So, let's swim!"

"No, I don't—I don't—"

"You don't what?"

He takes a moment, then makes a decision.

"I don't take my shirt off. Around other people."

My father's favorite quote—the one he recited to me every night before I fell asleep—was the simplest and hardest one of all. *In any moment of decision, the best thing you can do is the right thing. The worst thing you can do is nothing.* That one haunted me. *Before you act, it feels like a riddle or a curse. After you act, it feels like absolution and freedom. If you do not act at all, it is regret. Pure and simple.*

I set my book down and unbuttoned the top two buttons of my uniform shirt. Teddy looks up. I grab the bottom of my shirt and pull it up over my head. My skin tingles in the sunlight, still sensitive to heat and light after three years. The doctors said

I was lucky. Forty percent usually means your face is burned as well. But my scars hide under my shirt.

"You can touch it," I say.

I take his hand and rub his fingers across the scar tissue on my chest and stomach. It is fierce skin, tough skin, skin that has held together *in strenuous performance of duty*.

"It protects my heart," I say.

The sky goes white hot. The snow cone baby and the buffalo are long gone. The sun beats down on my bare back, and it feels good.

Teddy leans over to untuck the last part of his shirt that is still clinging to his uniform khakis. He pulls his shirt up over his head and tosses it behind him. The stretch marks are pink and veiny. They wrap around from his armpits to his boobs and from his love handles to his belly button.

"You can touch them," he says.

They are smooth. Scars inside his skin.

"They protect my fat," he says. His high-pitched little boy laugh becomes hysterical. Contagious. We get loud. And we don't care.

"Fuck you, Teddy!

"Fuck *you*, Rosie!"

I stand on the deck and proclaim to all of Copper Canyon, "It is a *fact* that Teddy Roosevelt would skinny dip in the Potomac with his trusted advisors and closest allies!"

I kick off my shoes. A neighbor's dog begins to bark.

"And as a symbol of that solemn solidarity and kindred camaraderie!"

"Don't do it," Teddy says.

Off go my pants.

"I hereby declare that we too shall skinny dip—right here in Lake Teddy—to honor the great Theodore Roosevelt and the great kinship and camaraderie that is right here between Theodore and Roosevelt."

I drop my underwear and dive into the water. The cold water shocks and stings then embraces. I hold my breath and wait at the bottom. A second later, still underwater, I hear an even bigger splash. We break the surface together, laughing and splashing. Total immersion. Complete the surrender.

"What the fuck are you doing!" Paul Ray is standing on the deck, looking down on us between our two piles of clothes. "Teddy, what the fuck are you doing!"

"We were just—"

"You shut the fuck up! I was talking to him!"

Teddy's gaze drops to the bottom of the pool. He walks to the ladder without saying a word. And climbs out of the pool. Paul Ray throws his uniform pants at him, "Put your clothes on, you little faggot."

* * *

When I get to my locker the following Monday, Tommy Stanick's stuff is gone. The note inside says his parents are no longer comfortable with him sharing a locker with me. It goes on to talk about HIV and the *tragic unknowns* of the disease.

On my way to homeroom, I see the first *Teddy + Rosie* sign written in lipstick on the boy's bathroom mirror. Michael Drostey makes kissing noises when he sees me in the hall. Ronnie Bootrie grabs himself and follows me until a teacher breaks it up. In one day, I went from the only Black kid at St. Agatha to *the only Black kid found naked in a pool with a naked white boy at St. Agatha*. Notes. Signs. Handwritten letters. All within the first three hours of my first day back. I become Rosie Palm. Rosie Bottom. All because Paul Ray didn't want people to think he was gay.

* * *

"I can't be here. Not today."

"How do you feel?"

"Please don't."

"Roosevelt—"

"I don't need your stupid questions or these stupid fucking stress dolls!" The stress toys fly. The candy bowl shatters.

"Stop!"

Her phone rings. She drops the call.

"You need to talk to me, Roosevelt."

"Where's Teddy."

"What happened to your book?"

She puts the file away and waits. "Where's your book, Roosevelt?"

I shake my head. "It was all bullshit anyway."

* * *

The hospital room smells like rubbing alcohol and cafeteria gravy. When I walk in, Teddy is asleep. His nose is packed. Both eyes purple with pooled blood. I sit next to the bed and hold his hand. His eyes flutter, then focus. He smiles.

"Let's go swimming," he says. "It'll be fun," he says. His laugh more of a congested exhale.

I nod. "Yeah. Bad idea."

"Hey, could you cover—"

I move his gown over to cover an exposed stretch mark on his left side.

"I got you this." I place a gift shop teddy bear on his tray. He nods. Smiles.

"In 1902," he says, "Teddy Roosevelt went hunting—"

"Mississippi," I say.

"Right. Mississippi. And his assistant—"

"Holt Collier," I say.

"Right. Tied a bear to a tree. But Roosevelt wouldn't shoot it."

"Because it was too easy," I say.

Teddy nods and shoots me with a finger pistol.

"Some people think that's just a myth," I say.

"I believe it," he says.

A nurse comes in to change the dressing on his forehead. She asks him if I should leave. He says no. She cleans the gash above his eye. Replaces his gauze and refills his ice chips.

I touch his face. "Paul Ray?"

He shakes his head. "Big Ray."

"Because I was naked in your pool."

"Because you were Black in my pool."

* * *

Over the next month, Teddy and I didn't talk. We didn't sit together at lunch. We saw Ms. Judi individually, and if we saw each other in the hall, we would turn the other way. Outside of teachers, neither of us spoke to anyone at school. In 1981, in Copper Canyon, if you were two boys swimming naked, you were fags who probably had AIDS. And there was no way to undo the damage that had been done. But from a distance, I would watch Teddy. I could see him healing. Getting stronger. His color getting better. The purple under his eyes fading to yellow. The mark on his forehead growing smaller and less pronounced. His scars becoming more obscure and invisible like stretchmarks under a school uniform shirt.

The last time I actually talked to Teddy, it was on the phone. I told him about my mom's new job with the state. About the house we found in Lansing and the school I would be attending next year. He said, yeah, a lot and wouldn't even say my name because we both knew that I was going to be anonymous in Lansing next year, and he was going to be the fat, possibly gay, X-ACTO kid, sitting by himself in Friends Group for the next two years. He was destined. And sentenced. And I was free. And neither of us understood it or deserved it.

* * *

On the last day of school, you could feel a restless energy building. For weeks, Tommy Stanick had been talking about a *fag fight* between me and Teddy. We were the drama. We were the gossip. The beef. And now they wanted blood. This was how it works. You didn't fight when you wanted to—you fought when *they* decided you would. All throughout the day, I heard about me and Teddy settling the score. Homeroom, lunch hour, fifth hour. You could hear the stories—how I came to his pool and tried to have sex with him. How he lured me into his pool to have sex with me. How we broke up, and now we hate each other, and the only thing left to do is settle it on the big lot behind the middle school gym, where all things like this get settled.

As soon as Mrs. Garko left the lot to have a smoke, a circle began to form around us. That's when I knew we were actually going to fight. That this was going to happen. Kids who never even talked to me were yelling my name, telling me to kick his ass.

Fag Fight! Fag Fight!

Tommy Stanick, waving his arms right in my face. Trying to get people to join him. They do. Ron Bootry and Michael Pawlick, still a little high from their walk to school, giggle and fall into each other as I pass. Someone takes my backpack off my shoulder. A group of seventh graders begin pushing me in the back, shoving me toward Teddy, who is now being pushed toward me, his belly heaving, his cheeks flushed red, his uniform shirt sweat-soaked and hopelessly untucked from his ever-descending khakis. We end up face to face. He still won't look at me.

"Fucking fight!" someone says.

A seventh grader pushes me into Teddy. He swings wildly. After all our lessons, he is still terrible. And they all see this. They see the fat kid. The kid with the X-ACTO. The one who swam naked.

He swings wildly again.

I slip and counter.

Teddy is off balance, out of sorts.

At some time in our lives, a devil dwells within us, causes heartbreaks, confusion, and troubles, then dies.

I drop my hands.

I show him my chin.

No man is worth his salt who is not ready at all times to risk his body—to risk his well-being—to risk his life—in a great cause.

Teddy pauses.

I scream, "Don't foul! Don't flinch! Hit the line hard!"

Teddy connects. Solidly. Beautifully. Right on the button. Just like I taught him. My hearing goes dull and watery. But I can hear them cheering. My vision goes soft and fuzzy, but I can see them celebrating. And as the seventh graders pick me up and pull me away, Teddy becomes something else.

* * *

This story first appeared in the After Dinner Conversation—January 2021 issue.

Discussion Questions

1. The first Roosevelt quote the narrator reads is, "Far better it is to dare mighty things, to win glorious triumphs, even though checkered by failure, than to rank with those poor spirits who neither enjoy much nor suffer much, because they live in the gray twilight that knows neither victory nor defeat." Do you agree with this statement? How does a person know if they are living this truth?

2. Do you think it is healthy (*or helpful*) that the narrator is so obsessed with Teddy Roosevelt? What role does Roosevelt seem to play in his life?

3. Teddy got put into the special classroom because he pulled an X-ACTO knife on the kids who routinely called him fat. What, if anything, do you think should have been Teddy's response to the daily taunting?

4. Before they go swimming, the narrator recites the Roosevelt quote, "In any moment of decision, the best thing you can do is the right thing. The worst thing you can do is nothing." Do you agree with this statement? Why or why not?

5. Do you think the narrator did a good thing by encouraging, then allowing, Teddy to hit him and knock him down? Is there another way he should have handled the situation?

* * *

The Hanging Man

Margery Topper Weinstein

* * *

The projections on the floor were making me dizzy, but I tried concentrating on my croissant. I didn't want the art to ruin my breakfast. I was alone among the art projections by unknown artists. The only single table among couples and families at a new event space not far from where I lived in New York City. It was meant to be a permanent installation of rotating unknown artists with the art projected onto the walls and moving on the floor as people ate coffee shop food.

"If you would just move your head. Just move," I heard a woman say to me from far away. But it wasn't far away. She was tugging on my purse. "Move because I can't see."

"There's nowhere to move," I said without bothering to look at her. I planned to get my money's worth and didn't want to miss the show for anything other than my croissant. "It's a table for two, but the other chair was taken away when they saw it would just be me."

"But if you could just move a little to the right or left," she whined.

"Then I'll be blocking another person's view, or my view will be blocked."

She muttered unintelligibly under her breath and kept whining to herself. I began to think of her as a little dog giving out little bark-grumbles because she didn't like her carrier. In fact, her grumbling to herself became a backbeat of the music we were listening to. I felt restful and meditative—until, out of the corner of my eye, I saw something swinging, dangling from a high rafter. It was a man hanging at the side of the event space. Unlike me, he wasn't blocking anyone's view. Maybe that's why no one noticed.

I turned to my right and left and backward. I kept getting to the point of opening my mouth to say something and then felt shy and stopped myself. No one but me noticed. Everyone's eyes were riveted to the wall, the floor, or the ceiling, where the images were projected. I felt embarrassed to interrupt their enjoyment. Even the woman who I guessed was the one who had asked me to move seemed too happy and at ease to disrupt.

I looked for security guards and found them alternating between watching the show and scanning the crowd. One bent down to ask a man to throw away a cup of whatever he was drinking, and another spent time searching the floor for garbage to collect. I thought I caught the eye of one and pointed toward the hanging man, but she shrugged her shoulders at me and looked away.

I tapped my phone to make an emergency call, but as soon as I did, a hand seized my shoulder. "No phones turned on or used in here," a man's voice hissed at me. "The light from your phone will ruin the show."

"It's just—just," I stammered.

"Shush!" he spat out at me. "Just be quiet. We're all trying to enjoy the show."

So I did. I reasoned that if I had noticed the hanging man, at least one or two others had. Why should I be responsible for taking action? How long could a person hang anyway? Wasn't he probably dead already? Nothing was going to change that. I watched the flashing colors and listened to the music from an opera I couldn't place.

Under my enjoyment of the moment, though, I was looking forward to the end of the show, which I thought would be a show unto itself, when the streaming crowd would leave the event space and, upon exiting, surely would see the hanging man. I even laughed to myself like it was a comedy I was about to witness.

The music never stopped and the lights never went on. It was a rolling show in which the credits rolled like at the end of a movie, but there was no other dividing line between one show and the next. You probably could sit there all day, and no one would notice you until the event space closed in the evening. There would be no mass exodus like there is from a theater after a play is over.

I was immobile at first, afraid to move. I knew that if I walked without stopping and left, I would have made a decision about the hanging man. I also was afraid that if I got up and left, I might miss the spectacle of others discovering the hanging man. So I sat. I looked away when a security guard walked past me. At first nothing happened, and then a few people stopped under the hanging man and pointed up. I thought I may have heard a faint scream, but it also may have been a whelp of delight.

I moved closer to the hanging man.

"Look at that!" a woman shouted, clutching her umbrella and pointing up. "Can you believe it? He hung himself—here."

"People hang themselves all the time. It isn't that unusual. I have an old friend whose husband hung himself. Lots of famous people have hung themselves. What's the big deal?"

"It's just—just—I've never seen a dead person before!" her companion shouted.

"What are you talking about? Yes, you have—tons of times. How many funerals have you gone to?"

"That's different—that's after they've been put together again and are ready for everyone to see them. This one's not ready."

I moved toward the exit, close enough to the hanging man to almost feel the bottom of his shoes grazing the top of my head. Two security guards were standing a few feet away. "Excuse me," I said softly and then more forcefully, "Excuse me!" One of the guards, who turned a toothpick around in her mouth with the tips of her very long fingernails, slowly turned to face me. She reminded me of a person emerging from a nap, trying to get her bearings. "Yes? What is it? Do you need something?"

"There's a man who's hung himself," I said, pointing upward.

"Him?" she nearly shrieked with hilarity. "He came that way."

"It's—he's—not a human?"

"Oh, he was—and he died—but not here."

"Where?"

She pointed out the door. When my eyes followed, she nodded.

"From the greater world? From where? I don't get it," I said.

"He's one of *them*," she said, pointing to a homeless man sitting on the corner with a sleeping bag wrapped around his lower body.

I shook my head slowly from side to side.

"They die every day now. Someone finds one of them dead, and the police sometimes take hours to get here to do something about it. I don't know who did it first, but one day, I came in here, and there he—a different one than this—was strung up. It became something extra interesting here. Got people talking."

"So, while you wait for the police, you string them up? Isn't that illegal? I thought you weren't supposed to touch a dead body if you found one."

"That's what I thought, too, but nobody seems to care. I think they're relieved to have them off the street. You know how it is, a dead body on the sidewalk, everyone stops to stare, and a crowd gathers around them. It interrupts things. Here it's just a thing some people notice and some don't. Some disregard it. They think it's part of the show."

I shook my head again, nodded, tried to half smile politely, and gave the hanging man a wide berth on my way out.

* * *

This story first appeared in the After Dinner Conversation—June 2023 issue.

Discussion Questions

1. Is this story social commentary? If so, what is the social commentary it is trying to make? Do you agree with the social commentary it is trying to make?

2. What would you do if you were the narrator in the story, and why?

3. Would you feel differently about the situation if some different dead things were strung up? For example, a dog, a cat, a sheep, a calf, a convicted criminal, or a child? If your opinion is different, why?

4. Why do you think the museumgoers see the dead man as part of the experience? Could a dead person in a museum be part of the art experience? Are there limits to what can be considered art?

5. How does the city you live in, and the homeless population in your city, change your perspective on this story? How does your opinion reflect your experiences and ethics?

* * *

Never Enough (Until You Earn It)

Keith "Doc" Raymond

* * *

Sbongo and Narita arrived. They made it. A long hard slog from their village in Uganda. Uganda betrayed them. Uganda killed her daughter and their parents. Al-Shabaab took their Indian mother and Ugandan father. Narita was a teacher, and they would have killed her, too, if they'd caught her. Caught them. They even evaded Ebola by traveling north.

But now they were free. After a dangerous sea crossing. After a year in a Turkish refugee camp, waiting for their papers to be processed for the EU. First, they were in Vienna, but the overcrowded city made them move on. Particularly because the Iraqis treated them with disdain. The brother and sister heard about greater opportunities in the west. They settled in Linz.

Finally, they were welcomed. They had a pleasant apartment with a view. People who could speak their language lived beside them, though they didn't know them. Plus, German classes for free! Not to mention a good income from the State. In Sbongo's mind, they set him up for life.

Narita had always been hardworking, so she went back to school. They gave her advantages she never had back home. Soon she was teaching again, and she was happy, being productive and making her own money. Prided herself when she dropped her state sponsorship.

Back in Uganda, Sbongo looked after their disabled mother. He enjoyed being home in those days, taking care of her and the animals. His father preferred to play cards with his friends and drink *waragi*. He used to cut hair on the street but found the gossip more entertaining than the shears.

Now in Austria, Sbongo lived a work-free lifestyle like his father. And with all the money he received from the State, he lived better than he had in Uganda, and no pigs to look after.

He'd walk up and down the *Landstraße*, the main street, all day, talking to acquaintances and making new ones. Basic income was all right. The way to go in his mind. If only other countries were not so greedy. If he or Narita got sick, they could go to a clinic or hospital and receive treatment for free. No barter, no exchange, and the pharmacy even gave them free medication. Well, sometimes he'd have to pay five euros, but hey, before he couldn't even afford that. Not to mention the cost of seeing a doctor!

If his mother were here, she'd probably still be alive. And no Al-Shabaab to threaten them. His friend Gonza asked him if he wanted to make extra money.

"Sure," said Sbongo, "what must I do?"

"Sell drugs. It's easy. They sell themselves."

"No, mon, I no sell. I don't want to be kicked out. Life is

good here."

Gonza ignored him after that. Besides, the *polizei* caught Gonza and sent him to prison for six months. No deportation. And he was back out on the street, selling in no time. Still, word was the government would deport you if you got caught too many times. Besides, selling drugs was work. Sbongo wasn't interested.

Instead, he heard he could get more money from the State if he found some girl, married her, and had many kids. Each kid added more money to his pocket every month. Having sex was not work and fun too. They'd pay him to do it, and their television wasn't so good anyway, so this was the best of all worlds.

Meanwhile, Narita's disgust for him grew. "Sbongo, what happened to your dreams? All the big plans you had. You told me night after night in the refugee camp how you wanted to open a restaurant. What happened to that?"

"Not interested, Sister. If I work, they take my money. Money I don't have to work for."

"And what's wrong with that?"

"Sides, no one is interested in African food. They want schnitzel and beer, not luwombo and spiced wine."

"That's just an excuse. Go! Make something of yourself."

"Like you? You're not making more than the State gives you for doing nothing."

"Yes, Sbongo. But I make it. It comes from my hand."

"Doesn't mean all that to me."

"Well, I'm moving out. Found me a man. We going to settle down."

"What about me?" Sbongo whined.

"What about you? Go live the dream, Brother."

* * *

When Narita left, Sbongo's day couldn't have been worse. The high fog was over the Danube, and the world turned gray. Few of his friends were out on the street. He was bored and frustrated. His plans to meet a girl weren't working out either. The girls he met liked one night with him or wanted money for the privilege. Then left him with a sneer.

Basic income wasn't carrying him as far as he liked, anymore. Even Gonza lived better than him. But the idea of work made him sick to his stomach. The apartment felt too big and empty without Narita. His dinner was no longer cooked and waiting when he came home. Sbongo wasn't lazy; he just never learned how to work, the discipline required to do a job day in and day out. To him, it was not such an important thing.

Despite this, he wanted to make a better life for himself. He thought about what Narita said and went to several restaurants, but no one wanted a man without experience. Then he met Ayaz. Ayaz ran a *kebap* shop that sold *döner* sandwiches and also slices of pizza. Ayaz not only offered him work but a better place to stay.

Sbongo was tired of the apartment he once shared with Narita. Too many memories. Plus, she wasn't returning his calls, so he accepted Ayaz's offer of a place and a job. He didn't know what he was in for.

Sbongo took the few belongings he'd accumulated and moved into the room behind the *kebap* shop. The entrance was from the alley in the back. He decorated his room with posters he found in a dumpster outside a movie theater.

Learning to make pizza and shave the *kebap* meat off a

rotisserie to stuff in a sandwich was a joy for Sbongo. He discovered a sense of fulfillment he had never had before. It was good work. But serving folks that stopped at the counter was his favorite part. Sometimes they would chat with him. It reminded him of his father's life.

He liked it. But not so much when they ignored him and texted or spoke on the phone. Those types would throw money at him like he was a begging dog after he gave them their food. What surprised him was that many of his friends no longer wished to spend time with him. They said he was too busy.

He had to admit he hated the hours. Getting up in the morning at a regular time was horrible. Ayaz had to bang on his door sometimes to get him moving. He enjoyed getting paid, though. The extra cash raised his quality of life. His German improved too. He could buy luxuries, like a TV, and order music CDs from back home. Music he missed.

Hearing the tunes made him homesick. If Uganda's leaders cared for their people, like leaders here in Austria did, he would still live there, prospering, living his life. He might even have his own family by now. Narita's daughter would still be alive, as would their parents. But it was not to be.

After a few months of the grind, the work became an endless nightmare of repetition. The highlight came when Sbongo saw his sister come up to the counter to order. It gave him a momentary glow.

It shocked her to see her brother serve her. "I'm proud of you, Brother. Making something of yourself."

He grinned.

"And this is yours?"

He wanted to lie, but he felt Ayaz's eyes on his back, even

if the Turk wasn't there in person. Instead, he said, "One day, maybe."

"You must come to our home. I will cook for you a proper matoke. You can meet my husband."

"I've met him."

"He's different when he's at home. You'll see. Here's my number. Call me, and we can plan, *ja*?" Narita said the last in German, breaking away from their mother tongue. It made Sbongo feel weird.

Narita left with her *döner kebap* and even gave him a tip. It soured his mood. He took it the wrong way. Felt insulted by her, even though she did it with love.

* * *

On the weekend, Ayaz drove him to Pleschinger Lake, to the north of the city. The large houses flattened his spirit. Sbongo thought he was living well until he saw those palatial estates. People dressed up, climbing into Mercedes Benzes, going to parties he could never attend, in houses where he was never welcome.

Sbongo couldn't understand why his basic income wouldn't allow him such a life. He expected it. They owed him that. He didn't realize these folks earned all the money needed to live their lifestyle. Sometimes it took their families generations to gain the wealth they now enjoyed.

The thorn in the rose stuck deeper when Ayaz said, "I have some bad news, my friend."

"What?" Sbongo growled. That drew a look from Ayaz.

"I've been paying taxes on your income. The city knows this, and the State is cutting your allowance. Not that it will make much of a difference because you have a place to stay and a good job."

Sbongo froze. Anger boiled up in him from his core. The State not only denied him the good life he saw all around him, but now that support was gone too.

Ayaz saw it in his face. The tremble in his hands. "Be happy. You make too much money. Enjoy living well, my friend. You are lucky. Many are not."

The State pulled the carpet out from under him.

"Say, let's go relax by the lake, enjoy the sun and the day. I'll buy you a beer," Ayaz finished. "It will help you forget your troubles, yes?"

* * *

Things went downhill from there. Losing his money from the State cost Sbongo half of his monthly income. He could no longer afford the luxuries he wanted. The lifestyle he carefully cultivated was dissolving. The dinner with Narita and her husband only made things worse.

She had a delightful house. And her joy weighed on him, particularly when she announced she was pregnant again. The food made him only more homesick. But there was no going back.

All these things he wanted for himself, he could barely afford anymore. The idea of taking on a girlfriend, not to mention a wife, seemed impossible now. His frustration grew. It became apparent in his attitude at work. When Gonza showed up asking for a slice, he shook a gold watch at him. His neck was gaudy with expensive bling. The girl at Gonza's side was a pretty Austrian, draped in fur, young, and no doubt from a privileged family.

It was the straw that tore him open. "Gonza, who are you

to order me around? You are a drug dealer. The worst of the worst. I do honest work here. Go away. Get out. Go get food somewhere else!"

"Hey, hey, hey," Ayaz said, "what is this?! He is a paying customer. You get out, Sbongo. You are done. Your poor attitude is costing me customers. Take your crap and leave. You're fired. You have no place here anymore!"

The blood drained from Sbongo's face. Especially when the girl said, "Look, he's gone white."

Gonza only made it worse. "Hey big man, you good man, go sleep in the park, boy. No more favors from me."

Sbongo's shoulders dropped. He slowly removed his white apron, dirty though it was, and folded it. He placed it carefully on the counter. His eyes met Gonza's one last time. Then he eyed Ayaz, still burning with his own anger. Sbongo walked to the back and grabbed his things, closing the alley door quietly behind him.

He slept in the park that night. And for the next two weeks. He simmered in his anger and despair. He smelled and was hungry most of the time. One night, it rained as he sat in misery. He could not face Narita nor beg for her help. Sbongo hated her husband and knew he would refuse him and be cruel. He wouldn't reduce himself and ask for help from them.

* * *

It was Halloween when riots broke out on the *Landstraße*. The night was young, and the voices of protest ugly. He joined the crowd racing toward the city center. Ahead, the *polizei* stood with clear shields, banging them with batons. The crowd energized Sbongo, intoxicated by the mob. He shouted slogans with them.

He didn't know what they fought for until he realized he was a stranger among them. They were primarily Arabs and Asians. Iraqi, Syrian, and Afghani, all refugees like him, and all better off because they still received basic income, and now they demanded more. Reading the signs they carried, he felt shame for the first time. They expected a better quality of life for doing nothing. It was then he realized he was no longer one of them.

He fell out of the crowd, drifting back against the buildings. It surprised him when he realized he was leaning against the *kebap* shop where he once worked. He turned and walked back toward the park with a new conviction.

The next day, he went to the *Gemeinde* office at the Burgermeister's building to apply for basic income. When the woman checked his citizen's number, she shook her head. "I see you have worked."

"They fired me," he answered, trying not to flinch.

"Then you must go to the *Wirtschaftkammer*, the business chamber. They will find you work or at least train you for a new job."

"But what about food and shelter?" Sbongo whined.

She shrugged. "Not my problem. Maybe they will find you something, *ja*. Now go."

The interview was over. Sbongo walked out and took the last of his money to get drunk. He sat in the park like an old derelict, feeling sorry for himself. The conviction he felt the night before faded. Bleary-eyed, he saw Gonza on the corner selling drugs to teenage girls who giggled and nuzzled him. He wanted to beat the crap out of the guy.

He told himself he'd go to the *Wirtschaftkammer* tomorrow. But tomorrow became the next day and the next. He begged on the street to get by. His self-pity grew with his beard. He smelled bad, worse than before, and the blisters on his feet became infected.

In the hospital *Unfall* clinic, emergency room, they sprayed him down with a hose because he stunk. Then told him to take a shower. They gave him soap, a thin towel, and some lost-and-found clothes that didn't fit him well. Finally, they cleaned and dressed his wounds and gave him a prescription for antibiotics.

The racist looks they gave him in the hospital didn't help. He traded the pills to a junkie for cash so he could get drunk again. He became another problem, not the solution in Linz.

* * *

Hitting rock bottom, he finally limped to the *Wirtschaftkammer*. They put him into a training position to do road maintenance. To his surprise, they gave him basic income until the end of his training period and put him up in a dorm with the other trainees.

Sbongo applied himself. His foreman, Gunther, was a jolly old Austrian with a potbelly. He told good stories about living in the Alps. They became friends.

Sbongo took the discipline he learned from working at the *kebap* shop and applied it to strengthening his work skills on the highway. Slowly, ever so slowly, he reacquired the pride he lost.

He didn't feel the pain when they took away his basic income at the end of his training period. Gunther insisted Sbongo join his crew permanently, and the *Wirtschaftkammer* gave Sbongo the assignment. He was making better money than ever before, and it made him feel good. He moved out of the dorms and rented an apartment. One better than what he had with Narita.

* * *

Several months later, Gunther invited him out to a restaurant on a Friday night. A local *beisel*, nothing fancy, an old place with good schnitzel and cheap beer. They sat drinking, eating, and sharing more stories. Gunther laughed heartily at Sbongo's jokes, and grinning, the Ugandan enjoyed a forgotten frisson of happiness he hadn't felt since he was back home, before Al-Shabaab and Ebola.

The woman serving them, wearing a *dirndl*, kept smiling at Sbongo.

"Oh ho," said Gunther, "I think she likes you."

"Nah, nah, I don't think so... she's just looking for tips."

"I think you're wrong there, my friend. I come here all the time, and she hasn't looked at anybody the way she looks at you."

Sbongo smiled; a warm feeling became a flush overwhelming the heat from his beer. Only then did he hear a couple arrive with a crying baby, distracting him from the server's wink. To his surprise, it was Narita, her husband, and their new baby. "Excuse me for a second," he said to Gunther.

"Go get her number, Sbongo," Gunther urged.

But he steered his way around the pretty woman toward his sister, who was just sitting down. The server followed him to the newly occupied table.

"*Grosse* beer, *bitte*," Narita's husband demanded as they sat down.

"And for you, Madam?"

"A soda *citronen*, soda with lemon."

Before the server left, Narita said to her, "You and my brother make a cute couple."

They looked at each other and blushed. Then both shook their heads, saying no, but possibly?

"Is that my new niece, Narita?"

"Nephew."

"He looks just like me!" Which earned him a dirty look from Narita's husband.

"You don't look like you are on basic income anymore."

Gunther, seeing Sbongo talking at another table, wobbled over. "He's not," he laughed. "Das ist only for losers, *ja*?!" Then slapped his belly. "Sbongo and I work together." Her husband noted Gunther's optical orange vest hanging out of his back pocket.

"Highway men?"

Sbongo and Gunther both laughed at the double entendre as the server returned with their drinks. She placed them on the table then pushed a napkin with writing on it into Sbongo's hand, whispering, "Call me."

* * *

This story first appeared in the After Dinner Conversation—May 2023 issue.

Discussion Questions

1. What is your opinion on the idea of basic income? Do you support basic income for the unemployed, refugees, or the unhoused? What, if any, requirements would you put on receiving basic income?

2. What, if any, obligations do you believe a country has to a refugee they knowingly accept into their country?

3. Do you think people naturally want to work for reasons other than money, such as identity, purpose, or pride?

4. In your opinion, what percentage of people on basic income would naturally look for a job, and what percentage would simply stay on it forever? What is the basis of your opinion, and what do you think is the difference between the two sets of people?

5. Do you think it is fair for people on basic income to protest because the amount they receive is insufficient for them to live with dignity? When someone starts earning wages, what, in your opinion, is the fair amount to reduce the basic income to?

* * *

Drag Brunch

Mark Bessen

* * *

On Friday, Kyle arrived in the crowded foyer of Swift's Attic in downtown Austin, itching for a bitch sesh. His friend, Jay, an unreasonably beefy muscle bottom he'd met on Grindr, waved him over to their table, where Kyle harrumphed into his seat. After the dumpster fire of a week he'd just had, he needed to extinguish the flames with some well liquor and good shit-talk.

"Can you believe this?" Kyle said, passing his phone to Jay over charred edamame and ice-ball cocktails. He'd just been uninvited from his soon-to-be-former best friend Hannah's bachelorette weekend via a text.

"It's just such a stupid excuse." Kyle popped a pale green bean out of its furry shell, busying his hands while his phone was otherwise occupied. "Saying she wanted a 'girls' trip.' So basic. Like, fifties housewife gender binary where's-my-dowry basic."

"Don't you hate weddings anyways?" Jay asked.

"That's not the point. *Tara* was invited, and Hannah doesn't even *like* Tara. And having her Maid of Honor tell me? She didn't even have the balls to tell me herself."

"Hannah has always been... The bottle blonde seeped in a little too deep."

"Sure, she like, drives a Mustang, but we've been friends for forever."

And they had. Even now, both thirty and on track to start their Real Lives—Hannah in some suburban enclave, Kyle in his apartment on Austin's east side—Kyle really thought they were closer than this.

"You're dealing with a lot right now," Jay said. "I'm just not sure this is worth your energy."

Kyle knew Jay was right. It *was* just a stupid bachelorette weekend. There was so much more important fucked-uppery in the world. Parents at the school where he taught tenth-grade English had petitioned to ban forty-eight books, citing concerns of "indecency, profanity, and egregious lewdness"—meaning, for the most part, they involved queer people; he'd just gotten back from sponsoring a student protest of a track meet because another district had banned a trans girl from racing, even though she wasn't very *good*; Texan politicians were on the news making vacuous arguments about grooming and protecting kids from drag queens instead of gun violence or climate change. The phrase "deviant lifestyle" had even reemerged in conservative politics like a bloodthirsty anachronism.

But it was all so abstract. What was he supposed to do, scream into the void about ideology? This bachelorette bullshit gave him something concrete to focus on. Rather than perseverate over the sweeping injustices beleaguering the Texas

Homosexual, Kyle could fix his ire on his morally bankrupt bridezilla ex-best friend.

"And Kyle, she treats you like her woke accessory. You thought you were her bff, but to her, you were always the gbf."

Straight girls sucked.

The bachelorette party would be leaving Austin for Miami soon. After Jay got up to go to the bathroom, Kyle started scrolling mindlessly through Insta until he saw a post from Tara that looked like something Pinterest had vomited up.

Hannah's Bachelorette Extravaganza!
May 3-5 • Miami Beach

Friday
7pm: Check in at Airbnb in SoBe, beys! Let the White Claws and tequila shots floweth!

9pm: Dinner rez at Nobu—she's serving fish ;)

Saturday
12pm: Brunch at Bacon Bitch—don't forget your sunglasses, bitch!

2pm: Beach day! Meet near the rainbow flag just south of 11th

7pm: Dinner at Santorini. Dress classy, ladies!

10pm: Gay clerbing! Start at Twist and see where we end up

Sunday
1pm: Drag brunch at the Palace!

4pm: Fly back to Austin :(

"Is this a fucking joke?" Kyle asked, his stomach clenching around soybeans and bourbon as Jay sat back down. Kyle showed him the post.

"Jesus," Jay said, shaking his head. "It's like they think they're going to the zoo."

* * *

The seven bachelorettes lounged around Gate 24 at Austin-Bergstrom International Airport, their bottom halves a mix of form-fitting Lululemons and retro Juicy sweatpants, matching pink T-shirts on top. Daniela's was printed with "Maid of Honor," the rest of the bridesmaids—Katie K., Tara, Caity C., Rebecca, and Sophie—labeled accordingly, and HRH Hannah's shirt said "Bride," set apart by gold glitter. They were wearing the T-shirts ironically, though, Daniela thought, no one else knew that.

Daniela, for her part, had enough self-awareness to be mortified by the gaucheness of the gaggle. She hated this kind of Live Laugh Love affair and suspected that even Hannah was a little embarrassed. Daniela had been surprised when Hannah asked her to be the Maid of Honor, assuming the role would go to Hannah's sister or her gay bff Kyle, and worried she'd been chosen less out of intimacy than logistical prowess since she worked as an event organizer.

Daniela recrossed her legs in the leather-on-metal airport chair and checked a few last-minute work emails, then set her Slack to "Out of Office." Good timing: her edible was just kicking in. They were all a little tipsy from the shots they had before they left for the airport. Daniela had stopped at one, but Sophie, the woo-girl of the bunch, had also covertly filled a flask with shots from the airport bar and was swigging from it now.

On her phone, Daniela looked over the itinerary that Tara had just posted to Instagram. Tara had volunteered to make the itineraries, and Daniela had been thrilled to offload a task, but she did wish she'd done a bit more quality control. All the drag references and gay slang felt like salt in the wound for Kyle, who she'd had to uninvite from the trip. She liked Kyle—he was real, even if he was sometimes insufferable. And Hannah's "girls' trip" excuse was flimsy at best. But what was she going to do? It was Hannah's gig. Hannah's mom was springing for the whole thing, so at least Kyle wasn't being put out. Daniela would honor her maidship, even if she begrudged it.

"Girl, let me see that rock!" said Rebecca, one of the bridesmaids who Daniela still struggled to distinguish. Rebecca grabbed Hannah's hand and let out a mock gasp. Then, she asked, "Where's Kyle?"

Fuck.

"Is he meeting us in Miami Beach?"

Daniela had forgotten to text the updated guest list to the out-of-towners on the trip.

Daniela looked at Hannah, who sat back in feigned calm and said, "I just thought he'd throw off the vibe, you know?"

Tara chimed in. "I've heard this drag brunch is epic."

Daniela was surprised by Tara's savvy redirection and worried she'd judged her too harshly. Her eye rolls would have been better directed at Sophie, who added, "I hear Ross Matthews goes there all the time."

"And Lisa Vanderpump." This was Caity C., who had auditioned for *The Bachelor* three times. "I wonder if any of the queens from *Drag Race* will be there."

"Have you seen the new season?" Rebecca asked. "The

queens are icon*ique*."

"It's so cool there's a straight queen!" Katie K. said. "I'm so glad the show is becoming more inclusive. He's so talented."

Daniela dug through her backpack for an Ambien, hoping to get some rest before they arrived in Miami—and to be unconscious to the flight attendant's raised eyebrow about their matching garb.

"Ugh, I'm so excited for our girls' weekend," Sophie said, apropos of nothing. "I'm *so* done with guys."

* * *

Hannah opened the door to the five-bedroom SoBe condo her mom had rented for them and let out a sigh of relief. She needed this: a good-vibes-only trip, time to relax and escape the wedding stress. This trip would be her safe space, free of judgment.

The girls looked around the gorgeous beachy rental—soft blues and whites, a matching set of glass coffee and kitchen tables, a stack of towels at the end of every bed—then paused when she saw the palm-tree-shaped floor lamps that Kyle had called "tacky bungalow realness but not a dealbreaker" when he'd helped her find places to stay.

She needed to get Kyle out of her head, or he'd ruin this weekend trip, his presence insinuating itself into every conversation like a phantom limb. Yeah, she should have told Kyle more than a week ahead, that was bad, but she just didn't have the energy for that kind of convo. And she knew it had been a dick move to make Daniela do the uninviting, but if Hannah had told him herself, he'd have asked for an explanation.

Some part of Hannah was a little sad that Kyle wasn't on

the trip—he provided endless, easy entertainment—but she was also a lot relieved. Kyle was a loose cannon (as he'd proven at that dinner with Trent), his words cannonballs aimed at creating as much wreckage as possible. She understood where he was coming from, and for the most part, she agreed with him, but she wasn't going to throw a wrench into her family dynamics. Hannah cared about social issues as much as anyone, but she wouldn't be a bitch about it.

"You okay?" Tara asked Hannah, extending a plastic shot glass toward her. Tara had already changed for dinner, which reminded Hannah she needed to get ready. "Seems like you're in your head."

"I'm fine," Hannah said. Tara was annoyingly perceptive but not terribly tactful.

"Are you worrying about Kyle?"

"Wedding stuff."

Not entirely untrue. Hannah had always intended for Kyle to be in the wedding, despite the ups and downs their friendship had weathered over the last decade. When she presented the list of bridesmaids to her wedding planner, a long-time friend of her mother's, Kyle had been on it as a brides*man*.

"Your mother was hoping for something more traditional," the wedding planner had replied, returning the amended list. "It would throw off the whole aesthetic—weddings are all about the pictures."

The bridal party would feature an ombré of matching dresses in descending hues of purple, from eggplant to pastel. Where would a tux fit in?

Hannah called her mother immediately.

"I'm not paying to have your grandparents scandalized," her mother said. "I don't think that's too much to ask."

Classic, Hannah thought, using money to enact her will—just like she had done to get her to go to SMU. Hannah had wanted to go to UT, but her parents didn't want their annual alumni donations to go to waste, so a Mustang she became.

"Remember, this wedding isn't just about you," her mother said.

Hannah started to protest, began formulating in her mind a speech about gender normativity and backward ideas. But she paused because, on some level, she shared her mother's ideal of the picture-perfect wedding. And also because Kyle had been a real headache lately.

What was she going to do, she thought now, as she applied her wingtip eyeliner, turn down the hundred grand her parents were paying for the wedding? She'd be better off having them pay, then donate twenty grand to the ACLU, or, like, Human Rights Campaign, if Kyle wanted to talk about "social impact." She just never found the right time to *tell him* he was out of the wedding party.

Hannah shut her worrying away with a snap of her makeup mirror.

"Okay, ladies," she said, waving her mom's platinum credit card. "Let's get some sushi."

* * *

Kyle slept on it, hoping he'd wake up purged of his resentments, but instead, they seemed to have multiplied in his subconscious, and he was fuming. He texted Hannah to see if they could talk, but no answer. He refilled his coffee mug from his French press, coffee grounds floating like bits of bark on the surface. He gave it until eleven before he called for the first time—noon for her, a reasonable hour. The phone rang six times and then went to voicemail. He texted again. Called again. By the third call, it went straight to voicemail. He wanted to give Hannah the benefit of the doubt—well, he wanted to murder her, but he also wanted to give her the benefit of the doubt—but he had to talk this out. They'd been best friends for *years*. Surely that warranted a conversation.

He went to Black Swan Yoga to try to sweat out a decision about how to handle it. As he flowed through sun salutations, he ruminated on his friendship with Hannah. She'd been the first to make him feel included at their shitty conservative high school. The first person he'd come out to. But had she just been looking for her Kurt from *Glee*? Was he really just the gbf, like Jay said, easy to cast aside when he became inconvenient?

They'd been fine until she started dating... *him*. Fucking Trent. That douchebro. He was a lawyer for the oil company Hannah's dad had worked for. Kyle had gone to dinner with them a couple months prior, bribing Jay into coming along. The four started off their dinner at Launderette with chitchat about the wedding and bachelorette party, which Hannah was late in planning. Kyle had suggested Miami Beach as a fun destination, easy to book last minute. At that point, Kyle had still been in the wedding party, but he still found the wedding small talk intolerable—and decided to address Trent instead.

"So," Kyle had asked, "how do you justify working for an oil company that is actively driving climate collapse? Is it really as simple as wealth accrual?"

"Whoa there," Trent said, holding up his hands. "Coming in hot."

Jay tipped back his cocktail.

"Kyle," Hannah warned.

"What?" Kyle said. "You said he was in the Federalist Society in law school. I figured he'd be up for a little debate."

"Hey, I'm socially liberal. I support gay rights. At least I'm not a Republican," Trent said.

"Oh come on, you're a lawyer. Don't pretend to be so obtuse as to think that fiscal conservatism is compatible with being 'socially liberal.' And you're a Libertarian, which is arguably worse."

"How is that worse?" Hannah asked.

"Because he thinks it's better," Kyle said.

He backed off after that Libertarian jab, for Jay's sake (well, and after a kick in the shin). Had that one dinner been what led her to uninvite him? He'd thought his friendship with Hannah was still on solid enough ground to weather political differences. At the time, he'd even thought, *Well, at least Trent's pleasant enough*—polite to waiters, perfectly fine at basic conversation. But with the benefit of hindsight, wasn't it actually *worse* that Trent was a nice guy? Somehow more nefarious that he smiled and laughed but spent his days making the world a worse place to live in? Even if he supported "gay rights," Trent had dropped the phrase "no homo" more than once, and that was with Kyle there. What did he say when there were no queer people there? And Hannah?—she just let it all happen.

Maybe Kyle had just been her gay pet. The fruit for the fruit fly. The hag's fag.

As he walked from yoga to the vegan kolache place, Kyle tried calling Hannah again. He considered calling Daniela but didn't want to use her as a messenger like Hannah had, that coward. So he called Jay, who was on his way to a shift at the airport, where he'd fly back and forth from Dallas until he worked his way up to a more optimal route.

"It's basically a millennial hate crime to cold call, you know," Jay said.

Kyle ranted about Hannah for a good ten minutes uninterrupted. He seethed about the encroachment of gay bars by entitled straight women. He couldn't even go to a drag show without fighting through a bachelorette party. Was no space sacred anymore? The same bridal parties that used gays as entertainment looked away—or worse, looked and said nothing—as queer folks systematically had their rights stripped away. Was the irony of celebrating *marriage* at a gay bar, when Obergefell was being debated in the news, lost on them? What a symbolically insipid institution marriage was. For fuck's sake, even watching *RuPaul* had gone from queer escapist fantasy to revenge porn now that it had been infiltrated by breeders. The latest season had a straight dude contestant—what?—just so the show could promote itself as having the first drag queen who couldn't say "faggot" without committing a hate crime?

Jay finally cut him off. "You know I, too, am a *homosexual*, right?" He pronounced it *home-uh-sec-shoe-uhl.* "Girl, either do something about it or get over it. Hang on, I'm going through security."

Kyle wasn't sure what there was *to* do, but he knew he wasn't good at just getting over things. Didn't he have a duty to stand up for himself? For the queer community?

Finally, Jay was back. "I don't know how to help you, girl." A pause, then, hesitantly, "But if you want, you know I can get you a flight out there."

* * *

On Sunday, the seven gals rented Citi bikes and rode along the strand past batido carts and thong bikinis until they arrived at Palace for drag brunch. As soon as they stepped inside, like gay magic, the whole party shifted dialect.

"Yasss queen! This is going to be uh-*mah*-zing!"

"Get it gurliez!"

"Werk bitch, those sunglasses are stunting."

Daniela heard it happen and started studying the program on the table as a reprieve from eye contact.

PALACE
Today's Queens!

Jenny Greg
When this fitness queen isn't using her -2% body fat to bench press bridesmaids, she's personal training at Gold's Gym (or in the steam room).

IG/Venmo: @JennyGregLifts

Daniela looked up when she heard the girls debriefing about the night before. They'd gone to Twist, the gay dance club they'd found on a blog about the best bachelorette party activities in Miami Beach, but things hadn't gone quite to plan. Neither of the Katies had gotten in because they were both wearing sandals (too many broken glass incidents, they were told), and Sophie was turned away because she started drunkenly screaming at the bouncer about the absurdity of such a rule in a beach town. The remaining girls were met with abundant side-eye once inside, and another bachelorette party at the club sucked all the energy out of the room as it colonized the dance floor. Still, that hadn't stopped Hannah's crew from wooo-ing until their feet blistered.

"The guys there weren't exactly friendly," Rebecca said, possibly trying to make the rejects feel better, but more likely having failed to read the room at Twist, Daniela thought.

"I mean, we need a safe space, too," Hannah added. "I guess that's the trade-off for not being hit on."

Daniela looked back down at the program.

Estefania Luz

She's back with a BBL and tits to match! Let's hope she doesn't sweat them pasties off! Or does. ;)

IG/Venmo: @Estefaniaaa

A waiter walked up to their table with a tray of mimosas, wearing the Palace uniform: tan booty shorts and muscle-tight T-shirts emblazoned with the restaurant's motto: *Every queen needs a Palace.* Almost all the waiters were Latino, and Daniela imagined them wondering what she was doing walking around with this flock of blondes.

"Oh my god, he's so cute," Katie K. said less-than-discreetly as the waiter walked away.

"What a waste!" Sophie whisper-yelled, already two shots deep and now searching for meaning in the bottom of her glass.

"Right? All the good ones are either gay or married."

"Or gay married!" Caity C. chimed in.

Sarah Tonin

As long as her Zoloft is slapping, Sarah's slapping back with original bops like Crying in a Wig *and* The Sunken Place (Between My Tits), *now available on iTunes.*

IG/Venmo: @SadSarahTonin

Three other bachelorette parties were seated throughout Palace, and Daniela was sure the brides were sizing each other up. One of the other brides had a picture of her husband-to-be taped to a popsicle stick. Was that a thing? Daniela looked over at Hannah, but she couldn't get a read on her expression behind her oversized Ray Bans.

Sophie waved the waiter back over and asked him how he kept his "badonkadonk" so tight. "A lot of squats and a lot of good sex," he said, humoring her by twerking in her direction before asking if she wanted a refill.

"Okay, read me, henty!" Sophie replied, holding out her glass.

Daniela cringed and dropped her eyes back to the program.

Tiara Monet
She's the dancing queen of Miami Beach, and she's ready to make your head spin.

IG/Venmo: @TiaraMonetMIA

Tonya Hardon
Watch out, or she'll break your shins and then fuck your boyfriend.

IG/Venmo: @ITonyaHardon

The girls ordered their breakfasts—a choice between

psychotically pink guava pancakes, chicken chilaquiles, or eggs benedict—all served with bottomless mimosas. No one ordered the pancakes—too many carbs—but Hannah added on a bottle of Veuve.

"Ugh, I just feel so at home here!" said Rebecca. "I'm basically a gay man trapped in a woman's body."

"Clearly begging to be let out," Hannah said, presumably aiming for snarky but landing on snide.

"A real gay Rachel Dolezal," Daniela added so that Hannah's comment wouldn't just float there, cruel and lifeless.

And your host, the legendary
Tiffani Phenomenon
She's been hosting drag shows since Stonewall, but she's still 39—hope you know your drag her-story!
IG/Venmo: @TiffaniThePhenom

Their food arrived concerningly quickly. The waiters continued to shuttle around pitchers of mimosas that they could almost balance on their perky derrieres. Daniela wasn't sure why she turned in the other direction, but she did, and she was the first to see him. *Fuck.* She didn't have time to intercept as Kyle walked into Palace and slid into his seat at the only table set for one.

* * *

Hannah did a double-take, hoping it was any other twink in a too-tight Target tee and six-inch inseam shorts, but it was Kyle, and he was walking up to her. As soon as she heard his piercing voice, the bubble of her blissed-out vacay weekend popped.

"Hi, Hannah," he said. "Can we talk?"

"What are you doing here," she said. What was this fake casual act he was pulling? He'd just flown out here and led with, "Can we talk?"

"You weren't answering my calls." Kyle wasn't gesticulating like usual, and his voice sounded off, freaky.

"Please leave." It took everything in her to keep her tone quiet. Icy.

"I'm going to watch the show."

"Come on, please? You flew all this way just to make me feel bad?"

"Why did you uninvite me, Hannah? Why'd you kick me out of the party?"

"You know, it's like, certifiable to fly all this way. It's fully unhinged. *Psycho*." She could probably call the police and have him arrested for stalking.

"Come on, Hannah. Be real for once."

"Why do you care so much?" Hannah asked. "It's a bachelorette party. You hate weddings."

"Because we were best friends for years. Because I cared about you. I *loved* you!"

As Hannah heard Kyle deploy the past tense, she realized she'd been using it for years.

"Kyle, come on, I'm not going to do this here. Now."

"Fine. Save it for that homophobic neofascist melted Ken doll that Daddy picked out for you."

He knew how to jab right where it hurt. Two years ago, her father told her he had colon cancer, and six months after that, he was dead. But not before telling her, "Trent is a good man," and to Trent, "Take care of my Hannah." Shortly after, they'd gotten engaged.

"Jesus, Kyle, is this how far you've slid? You're such a social justice warrior now you can't even tolerate the idea of people you disagree with?"

"He voted for Trump!"

"That doesn't by default make him a neofascist. You can't hold every individual accountable for, like, big systemic failures." She huffed. "I'm not having this conversation," Hannah said.

"Classic. Whatever. I guess it makes sense that you'd want one last hoorah before you settle into suburbia with that where-were-you-on-January-sixth, nazi-paraphernalia-collecting oaf. And the drag brunch? The gay clubbing? All of it's just entertainment for you, huh? What, did your dad know RuPaul through fracking or something?"

"Don't fucking talk about my dad."

Her friendship with Kyle had been on life support for years. It made them both look too closely at themselves through each other's eyes—her, a fair-weather liberal, an apologist for conservatives; him, a moralistic bullshitter too convinced of his own oppression to give people a chance. Now, they brought out the worst in each other, which was its own strange and powerful intimacy. Like seeing someone without any skin, their network of nerves exposed, radiating pain at the slightest breeze.

Hannah took a breath. "Kyle, we haven't been 'best friends' in a decade. We were in *high school*. You're too fucking much now. You've *always* been too fucking much. You drag everything down around you. You have to *stop* with this holier-than-thou bullshit!"

Just then, the hot, muggy air thickened with the clapping

of wooden hand-held fans, the waiters creating a mechanical chorus that silenced the restaurant. The silhouette of a three-foot beehive wig appeared in the dressing room door, and Palace erupted into applause.

* * *

The table of bachelorettes shifted uncomfortably to make room for Kyle, who was forced into a seat among the party to avoid disturbing the show. The energy between him and Hannah was enough to break Florida off the continent and send it drifting, dick-shaped, into the sea. He felt himself clutch the stem of his mimosa flute like a dagger. He wanted so badly to hurl the sticky elixir in Hannah's face, to watch the orange juice drip out of her overly bleached hair, hair the color of complicity and gentrification and gay best friends, to right the scales of justice by a couple ounces at least. Instead, displaying heroic restraint, he tipped his glass back into his mouth and gestured for a refill. Then another.

Kyle's stomach churned as Tiffani Phenomenon floated down the aisle to the front of the room like a seven-foot-tall linebacker walking en pointe, a huge sequin purple train trailing behind her.

"Oh my god, is that Bob the Drag Queen?" asked Caity C.

Rebecca delicately corrected her, saying they just had similar makeup, but Kyle knew the only thing Tiffani had in common with Bob was her skin tone.

Kyle drank some more, then focused his attention back on Tiffani as she announced the performers. A queen in knee-high bright-pink stripper heel boots held together by matching duct tape climbed up a structural support pillar and death-dropped eight feet to the ground. Even through his velvet rage,

Kyle gay-gasped. The next danced an athletic salsa, culminating in so many in-place cartwheels Kyle felt like he was staring into a windmill. Estefania Lux racked up tips by dancing with the bride at another table, twerking her BBL'ed ass on the bride, then twerking away when the bride grabbed what she presumably thought was a breastplate but was actually Estefania's tit, as revealed by a burlesque number ending in nothing but tasseled pasties. To get through all of it, through the *yas queens* and *werk hentys* and *oh no she betta don'ts* from the crowd, Kyle searched for the bottom of his bottomless mimosas.

After half an hour of dancing numbers and lip syncs, Tiffani was back in the center of the room, announcing an intermission to refill drinks and take out more cash for tips. Now was his chance. Kyle stood up, walked over to Tiffani, and slid the bedazzled mic from her acrylic claws.

"I've got something to say," he said.

"This isn't an open mic, honey," Tiffani chided to hesitant chuckles from the audience. "Come on down from there." But Kyle was already climbing onto the table he'd abandoned, ready to deliver his polemic from this makeshift pulpit.

"I've got something to say," he said again, gathering his thoughts in a final swig of mimosa, his vision blurred and his moral certainty coming into focus.

"Let me tell you something about appropriation," he began. The audience groaned, but he went on. By the time Kyle would board his plane in a few hours, aching and ashamed, it would all blur together. But he remembered talking about the bachelorette party drag show industrial complex. The antiquated, patriarchal financial institution of marriage. The banned books, the bathroom bills, the slow trans runner who wasn't even allowed to lose. "And this fucking minstrel show?" he added—this he would regret later, reflecting on how Tiffani had put her hands on her padded hips in the Tik Tok video—"All these talented queer people performing their art for a bunch of drunk bridesmaids, and you're handing out *ones*?"

Then, as the waiters and queens mulled around below him, some snapping along and others with arms crossed, he turned to Hannah. The purportedly well-intentioned suburban white girl, the most insidious of them all, just out there collecting her tokens. But just as Kyle was about to reach his apotheosis, to bridge the gap between personal and political, to connect this drag brunch to the broader systemic flaws it represented, his foot slipped off the edge of the table.

As he tumbled to the floor, Kyle's eyes met Hannah's, and he saw that she was a stranger to him now, maybe always had been. She just stood, frozen, watching the show. Tiffani lunged forward and broke Kyle's fall, his head landing on her glittered arms and his gaze on the ceiling, which was painted with a re-creation of the Sistine Chapel. But here, Adam had been rendered as a muscular jock, blessedly better endowed, his outstretched finger reaching toward a long purple nail that, when Kyle traced it back to its source, revealed that God herself was a drag queen.

* * *

This story first appeared in the After Dinner Conversation—November 2023 issue.

Discussion Questions

1. Hannah's mother refused to give her $100,000 for the wedding and bachelorette party if Kyle was a bridesman. What should Hannah have done in response to this threat? Is Hannah allowed to be self-focused on her wedding day?
2. Can morals be implemented sporadically, or must they always be followed? Could Hannah have excluded Kyle from the wedding but donated $20,000 from the wedding coffers to the Human Rights Campaign and have that be considered a moral compromise?
3. Given the story's facts, how would you describe Hannah's support of LGBTQ equality?
4. What should Kyle have done in response to being excluded from the bachelorette party? Does he have a duty to stand up for himself and the queer community by flying to Miami to confront Hannah with her hypocrisy? Is that why he is doing it?
5. Are drag shows, minstrel shows? If the majority of the people in a drag show are straight, does that then make it a minstrel show?

* * *

What We Talk About When We Talk About Reincarnation

Edward Daschle

* * *

My boyfriend, Mike, was talking, just really going on like he was delivering a lecture in one of his economics classes. He's twice my age, so he thinks that gives him the right.

Our friends call us Michael squared when they think they're being cute, but we're safe around Jaime and Amy since their names rhyme. Amy was my friend, and Jaime was Mike's, and it was the two of them who'd introduced the two of us, though not with any intention that we'd begin dating. We were just two guests at the same party they'd been hosting. Sometimes I felt this, more than anything else, was what kept us all as a set. There was little else we really had in common. Mike and I only drink wine, but since Jaime and Amy brought the drinks, what we had was beer. The bottles we'd already emptied crowded the table under the light, and I was trying to decide if they were amber or just brown while Mike got himself worked up over the history of reincarnation. He'd made his way through literature and metaphysics and ended up in a cul-de-sac of science fiction. He doesn't believe in anything he calls woo-woo or what anyone else would call spiritual, though there is a little Buddha nestled between a few books in the living room.

The apartment is Mike's, and his furnishings are to die for. I don't remember what we ate or drank the first time he invited me over, but I do remember the mid-century modern Danish chairs, futon, and cabinet, the tastefully minimalist, queer paintings, and the small statement sculptures on his shelves and the coffee table. His, I recognized in this first glimpse, was a life well-organized and not one spent on anyone else. He had constructed himself, too, in a way, through daily workouts and tight shirts, a neatly trimmed beard to deemphasize his age, and the gold-rimmed glasses he preferred over contacts. When we officialized our relationship by telling our friends and touching each other delicately in public the way couples do, he became my safety net, a personification of the concept of security. Already, I'd been thinking of him as something of a template for who I'd like to become. I'd decided, not so explicitly at first, though certainly it was a decision, once I reach his age, once he's passed and I have my own apartment overlooking the water and a boyfriend half my age, I will shorten my name to Mike and carry on his legacy of good taste.

"Hey, who do you think you were in a past life?" Jaime asked.

It took all of Jaime's burly force to interrupt Mike. Jaime was built like a Tolkienesque dwarf, looking as though nobody would ever be able to push him over. He'd transitioned only recently. Sometimes I guiltily felt that talking to him was a pronoun minefield, though on the couple occasions I slipped up, he said nothing. For a brief period when I was younger, I thought I might like to be a girl. I'd never told anyone this, and it didn't matter, because I did not feel that I was trans or at least not that I could live as a trans woman. It was just an idle thought, and I figured if there were an afterlife where I could choose how I would turn out in my next life, I would probably not choose to be a boy again. Biologically anyways. I wondered if it was fucked up to think along these lines, if this reinforced the notion of who was a real woman and who wasn't, but I wasn't about to have that conversation here, not now. It wasn't a beer conversation, something so delicate. Maybe it was a conversation I could only have with a therapist since Mike would condescend, not cruelly, but only out of years of experience in entertaining fruitless hypotheticals and out of his own misgivings over the complexities of gender identity.

Jaime said that in a past life, he figured he was nobody special. He'd never won any awards growing up—the only statistically unusual thing about him being the fact that he was a trans man. He'd probably worked, ate, shit, and then died of something stupid like a toothache.

"Though considering I have you now, I must've done something right in my last life," Jaime said to Amy in a voice that sounded like he was talking to a dog. Though I hadn't yet said it aloud, I did love Mike, but I would hate to hear my own voice dribble so mushily from my mouth.

"I think in a past life, I was Galileo," Amy said.

"Galileo?" Jaime asked.

"I just think I have a connection to him; I did a report on

him in first grade."

"What?"

"On Galileo, Michael, you remember, right? We had to choose a scientist, and then our teacher was fired for spreading secular beliefs."

I laughed.

"No, I don't remember any of that," I said, "but that's kind of hilarious. I can't believe they fired, what was her name—Ms. Miller, right?—over something like that."

"You can't?" Mike asked. "I can believe it completely."

"You know what I mean. Sure, it was a Catholic school, but seriously, besides the uniform, it was more or less normal, I think," I said. "And I don't know, things like that... they just always seem to happen somewhere else."

I looked around at the others. Amy shrugged.

"But why Galileo?" Jaime asked. "I mean there's more to it than a report, isn't there?"

"It's stupid, but I guess he just always sort of stuck with me. He's like my own personal inspirational quote. Like 'hang in there, Amy, at least you aren't imprisoned,'" she said.

I laughed again, but Jaime, I could see, looked thoughtful.

"But you were imprisoned in a way," Jaime said. "You had to hide yourself. I basically had to break down that closet door with an axe."

"And I'm glad you did," Amy said, tilting her head gently so that it touched Jaime's. "But I don't want to blame my parents for that. I mean, they gave me everything and they loved me, even if I couldn't always, you know, say everything to them."

Jaime wrapped an arm tightly around Amy's shoulders, pulling her into his side.

Amy's parents adopted her when she was old enough to be grateful but young enough not to be bitter about the whole system. We've had conversations about what that means to her. Once, she told me how she had this feeling that if she wasn't perfect, they'd get buyer's remorse and question her adoptee warranty. It was why she'd taken longer than I had to renounce the faith in which we'd both been raised. She still considered herself to be a spiritual person, and sometimes her social media posts made me wonder if she didn't need something to fill the space the church had left behind.

"You are perfect. Anyone who could reject you just doesn't know you," Jaime said.

Mike, I could tell, wanted to say something. Maybe how that wasn't true. How there were plenty of people who would reject you because they knew you, but I reached across and squeezed his thigh gently to shut him up. He set his warm hand on mine.

"All right, Mike, let's hear it," Jaime said smugly and resignedly, ready it seemed for something long-winded. He was leaning back again, the thin-armed chair looking entirely too delicate to contain his swagger, the empty beer bottles before him forming a crenulated parapet. "And I don't want to hear any sort of theory or anything like that. Just pretend, for a moment, that reincarnation exists in the way most people understand that it does."

"Fine, fine," Mike said, in that fake exhausted voice he sometimes uses, the voice I hate because it reminds me how much older he is, how in the wrong light he looks like my dad. "Actually, my first boyfriend totally bought into all that spiritual bullshit. This was back in the early '80s when things like psychics were on their way out, barely holding onto the market share they'd scratched out for themselves in the '60s and '70s. I was a skeptic, but I was also smitten, just over the moon for him. He was so brave and out there and sexy too. I'm not ashamed to say he was my first love, and first love really makes you do crazy things. I was practically a different person from the bitter old faggot you see before you now. What I mean is, I was willing to believe anything he believed in, no matter how crazy I really thought it was.

"So he had this psychic he went to, and one time he took me to see her. She had on all this eye makeup and loads of shawls and things. At the time, I thought she was really old, though now I think that was just the effect she was going for— you know, to make herself seem wiser and more mysterious— she probably wasn't much over forty at the time." Mike lifted his beer to his lips, but didn't take a drink, just held it there before his face almost as though he'd been petrified, the Medusa gaze of memory holding him fast. I held my own second beer, though I'd already decided I wouldn't finish it, not with all those empty calories. I couldn't afford them, not if Mike was going to think about an old boyfriend. I didn't like the look he had in his eyes. Or maybe I was just jealous he wasn't looking that way at me.

He blinked, took a drink, and then set the beer back on the table.

"He asked her to tell us about our past lives, if we'd been lovers then like we were at the time. Apparently, this was the main service she provided. Anyway, she told us that she saw something—she put on this misty voice—and for his sake, I really tried to let myself buy into it. Later though, after the first time we broke up, I promised I'd never pretend to believe in bullshit for a guy again, no matter how hot he was. I did, I believed in a lot of bullshit, but I got more suspicious each time. She said why yes, the two of us were, but things ended tragically.

"Maybe she knew fags loved melodrama, or maybe she was picking up on something else, but that really got him, and me too by proxy. She said we'd been in boarding school together in the 1910s. We had a clandestine relationship. He'd had to put off the girls his parents tried to set him up with, and I was always finding new ways to sneak into his room when his roommate was out. Very *Maurice* and *A Separate Peace*. But then the war started, and there we were, me English and him German—it could've been the other way around, but I guess she noticed a sort of Teutonic intensity in him, which is probably why she was in the business she was in, the way she picked up on things like that. We fought on opposite sides of the war, memories of each other were all that kept us alive in the trenches. But then, when in the heat of battle, we didn't recognize each other, all covered in trench mud and wearing our uniforms, we fought, and I killed him. Only as he lay dying in my arms did I realize who he was. I died not long after from sepsis or something else ugly and painful.

"That's what she told us, anyway."

"I'm going to have to talk to that psychic," Jaime said. "Do you think she's still alive?"

"I don't know," Mike said. "But Harvey died seven years after that."

We could hear the rush hour traffic on the street far below, but that was all we could hear. I kept expecting someone to break the silence before realizing it had to be me. "How did he die? You've never talked about him before."

I felt so impotent. I was always thinking about how even if our relationship ended with Mike's death of old age, barring unreasonable longevity, we would be together for less than half his life. It's disconcerting, sometimes, to think how long I'll be left alone.

"How do you think?" Mike asked, but the gruffness was only playacting. It was a bad actor's attempt at putting on the anger the script asked for. It was well-worn and cliché.

"So, it was AIDS," Jaime said, and I could see Amy tense up beside him. "That fucking sucks. It's always fucking AIDS. You know, my uncle died of AIDS. I was young when he passed; this was in the early '90s. I just remember him being all thin, pale, and wrung-out looking. His lips were dry and looked like the Salt Flats in Utah near where my grandparents lived. I was certain he'd been cursed since I was really into mummies at the time."

"It's always fucking AIDS," Mike agreed. "He died in '89. I don't really want to get into everything, but it was just as terrible as you're imagining. I wasn't there as much as I know I should've been, but I was young, and all he was doing was dying. He didn't have any family with him either; they'd decided to forget him before we even met. When I did visit, he just kept repeating that bullshit story the psychic told us. I think that's why I still remember it. There were times when I was certain he couldn't tell the difference between what was real and what was the story. He didn't just believe that he'd lived that past life; he believed he was living it out in that hospital. He even tried to speak German a few times. But he didn't know German, so he just muttered a few made-up phrases in the worst fake accent I've ever heard. I had to work so hard not to laugh, even with all those men dying around him."

The sky began to orange and then purple, blooming like a flower or like a bruise, considering the topic of the conversation. Mike's furniture cast spidery shadows across the floor, and just for a moment, before Jaime shifted, the light caught in the empty bottles on the table, refilling them.

"What month did he die?" I asked.

"What month...?" Mike asked, still smiling off the end of his sad laughter. "It would've been... August? Yeah, fucking terrible month. He thought he was freezing to death, but I was boiling in that shitty apartment we used to share."

"I was born in September that year," I said. I was speaking quietly because even as I spoke, I knew I probably shouldn't be saying what I was saying. But I couldn't help it; the topic of the evening had caught hold of me. "You know how that psychic was talking about lovers in past lives? Maybe he was my past life, and that's why we're..."

Mike stared at me, eyes seeming to reach right to the edges of his gold-rimmed glasses.

"You know, I just thought there would be something magical about that, and considering the coincidence," I said, "of when he died and I was born... it just fits, I guess."

We stopped breathing, all of us. Amy and Jaime were still; Mike stony beside me.

"It's all bullshit," Mike said finally without force. "The psychic, reincarnation, all of it. And I hate the idea of soulmates. The world's too big for soulmates and any of that bullshit. You shouldn't need to believe someone is your only choice to fall in love with them. You should just be able to love or lust or whatever else. I mean, Jesus Christ, none of that is necessary. It's just about compatibility and making it work. Fighting to make it work if you have to."

I set my hand back on Mike's knee, and though his body was warm, all I felt was coldness when he didn't set his hand on mine.

"Soulmates scare me," Amy said.

"How do you mean?" Jaime asked.

"It just seems so easy for two people to never meet and then your souls would never be fulfilled. I mean, sorry Michael, but Mike is twice your age. I don't think you ever expected to end up with him. And what if there are rules to soulmates we don't know?"

"Jesus," Mike muttered. He was done with the conversation.

"But maybe that's what reincarnation is all about," Jaime said. "Correcting mistakes made by another you in another life. Maybe we just keep coming back until we find our soulmates."

"Or maybe it doesn't mean anything at all, and it's just something our ancestors made up because their lives were shit, their world was shit, and every day they were starving and depressed," Mike said.

The cats screamed just then from the bedroom.

"Oh, shit, forgot to feed the bastards," Mike said and went to let them out. We always keep them in the bedroom whenever we have guests over, even, or maybe especially, guests who like cats. It's not that we're concerned about the cats being a nuisance, they are nice enough as far as cats go, but guests are always making a nuisance out of themselves around cats. Some people are allergic to cats, but the real issue is how the cats derail conversations. They come into the room, and there we go spending an evening talking about cats instead of whatever it was we were talking about before the cats entered the picture.

And in they came, mewing up at each of us. Jaime nabbed the orange one we called Marmalade when we weren't calling him Stinker, and though Amy wiggled her fingers at Alfredo, he sauntered off into the kitchen after Mike, more interested in food than attention for the time being.

"You know, cats have nine lives," I said.

"So they say," Jaime said while he scratched behind Marmalade's ears. "Hey, can we get...?"

"Hey, Mike? Can you grab a few more beers? So, is it reincarnation," I asked, "when a cat dies, and they use another life? Or is it more like Mario, and they just get to try again?"

"I hadn't really thought of it that way, but now that you mention it, I guess I would probably say it's more like Mario," Amy said.

"But what if it were reincarnation?" I asked. "How many cats are actually running about in the world? I mean, how many have there ever been?"

"Nine times fewer than we think, I guess," Jaime said.

"No, but seriously," I said, "what if reincarnation doesn't obey the laws of space and time, you know? I mean if we're going spiritual anyways, there's no reason to believe that a cat with nine lives has to live those lives back-to-back like dominoes. Oops, got ran over, there's one down. Oops, got eaten by a coyote, there's another—"

"Michael," Mike warned as he returned to us with what would turn out to be the last round of beers. He's sensitive to talk about the cats dying. He grew up in California, where his family had practically been feeding the coyotes with the cats they brought home from the shelter.

"So, Mike's—our—two cats might actually be the same cat reincarnated into the same place and time in two different bodies," I continued. "In a few years, when one... passes... it will go on to the great kitty beyond and then get its next life and reincarnate a few years before now as the second cat. Just like that. Or maybe one cat is the first life, and the other is the seventh or something. So maybe the sixth life experienced the end of the world or was a sabretooth tiger."

Marmalade leapt from Jaime's lap to join his brother in the kitchen.

"You know, I kind of lied earlier." Amy admitted.

"What about?"

"About who I thought I was in a past life. I mean, about why I thought I was who I was," she said. "I did do a report on Galileo and all, but actually it has more to do with that Indigo Girls song. I went to one of their concerts with an ex—sorry honey—and I felt like I was experiencing destiny. Like I did a report on Galileo, and there they were singing about him."

"Oh fuck, major lesbian credentials alert!" Jaime said, jabbing the air repeatedly with his index fingers like an insistent sign pointing Amy out.

"Destiny and reincarnation? I feel like there's something there," I said.

"Actually, hey, I have a theory. My theory is that having a child is the closest thing we have to reincarnation," Jaime said. I noticed he and Amy exchanged a meaningful look.

"Really? Come on," Mike said. "That's so hetero. It's such a straight belief to think that having children is anything like reincarnation. It's completely toxic. My parents had that sort of feeling about me and then hated when I didn't turn out just like them."

"You know I actually don't disagree with you there?" Jaime said, and Amy nodded. "Like it's fucked, yeah, but I was thinking more biologically speaking. There's genetic memory and all that shit. I read something about how stress can be passed down through generations."

"Plus, you're talking about expectations, right? Not really reincarnation," Amy said. "My parents aren't my biological parents, but they had expectations."

"Sure, fine," Mike said. "But it's still fucking hetero to think of your child as any sort of extension of you. They aren't beholden to you. Like do you think you owe your past lives anything? I mean, obviously not because reincarnation isn't real, but it's the same with children. Just let them be their own person. Maybe we should just stop having kids for a bit, like as a society, until we get our messed-up shit sorted out."

"You're going to hate this then, but Amy and I have something kind of big to tell you."

Jaime loves saying he has something big to tell you. Those were the same words he used to come out as trans, and likely how he'd announced he was a lesbian in a previous life, years before he and Amy started dating. But, though occasionally he chases this phrase with truly momentous news, mostly it's exaggeration, and we all get to roll our eyes at his idea of scope.

"We're planning to get pregnant," he said.

Mike and I didn't have to exchange looks, though in a sitcom, we would have, very urgently and dramatically. We'd both been blindsided, and neither one of us knew quite what to say about this.

"Congratulations!" I said.

"Living that hetero fantasy!" Mike said. "Fantastic!"

"That's not—" Amy said.

"As a queer couple, anything we decide to do is inherently queer," Jaime said. "Anyways, I'm the one getting pregnant."

"Yeah, okay, okay," Mike said. "Oh, wait, hold on, back it up. How's that?"

"I've always wanted to be a mom," Amy said, tone halfway between apologetic and staunch, "but getting pregnant, going through all that, and then the time I'd have to take off from work... it just doesn't appeal to me. But you know, before Jaime came out, we weren't considering having a kid at all. It wasn't even on our radar."

"It's because I wasn't being who I am yet, if that's not chronologically confusing," Jaime said. "I had to kill whoever that bitch was—"

"Honey," Amy said lightly. She'd fallen for that bitch after all.

"Sorry, but I mean, going back to reincarnation again," Jaime said, picking up his empty bottle, not remembering he'd already emptied it. "I couldn't even conceive of being a parent in that past life because being a parent meant being a mother. But now, my soul and mind are aligned, and I can be the father I was always meant to be."

"Soul and mind," Mike repeated with a hint of derision, whether over the spirituality of the sentiment or over the absence of "body" in the equation. "But you're a man now, right?"

"I've always been a man," Jaime said. "It just took me some

time to figure myself out."

"Hmmm," Mike said and finished off his third beer.

"What?" Jaime asked.

"It's just you were a lesbian, and now you're planning to have a kid, so was it really always?" Mike asked. They'd had this sort of discussion before to varying degrees. When Jaime came out as trans, Mike had had any number of questions, only a few of which he'd asked Jaime and a few more he'd ranted about to me later. He was from a different generation, I'd explained to Amy, the two of us acting as wartime negotiators when our partners argued over identity.

"Don't give me that bullshit," Jaime said. Amy's fingers jolted in a warning caress across Jaime's shoulders. "Look, identity's fluid, and we're all always just trying to figure ourselves out. I mean, come on, dude, no need to be transphobic."

"Transphobic? What the hell," Mike said. He never raises his voice just increases the pressure. "I'm the fag who lived through the AIDS epidemic here. Look, I'm just saying you can't have it both ways. You can't expect people to think of you as a man if you plan to get pregnant. And hey, this isn't really about you. I'm just tired of people making up new identities now because they want to be special. We didn't live through all that bullshit so that the next generation of dykes and fags could find new ways to be discriminated against. Jesus Christ. You can be a masculine lesbian without being trans. Identity doesn't have to be so binary as—"

"Fucking binary? I'm a man, and I'm having a baby! Fuck!" Jaime shouted, though he was still leaning back in his chair.

"How would you define a man then?" Mike asked. "Can

you even define a woman anymore?"

"If I started to define *woman*, you'd just pull out a plucked chicken and say 'behold, a woman!'"

I laughed. Somehow, I was laughing. As much as I didn't want to push on Mike's ego or test the already strained flex of the evening, I was laughing, imagining a woman-sized plucked chicken, taking calls in an office, walking about in heels, wearing lipstick. As though heels and lipstick were what anyone might use to define a woman.

"Sorry," I said. "I was just imagining..."

They were all looking at me, and for a moment, I wondered if this would be enough. Mike always apologized in the end when he went too far—he was always taking things as far as he could. But even so, I wondered when the end would be too late, when Jaime or Amy would decide to put the story down before they got there, and if too late might've just passed us by.

"Jesus," Mike whispered. And then looked back up at Jaime, earnestness in his eyes. "Hey, congratulations on the whole baby thing. Forget I said anything. So how are you doing it? Are you going to bust out the old turkey baster?"

He'd toted out that old gag, the clumsiness itself an attempt at an apology.

"You know, it's getting late," Jaime said. "We should get out of here."

"Oh, come on," Mike said. "It's still rush hour. Stay a bit."

"I have this great aged cheese I found at the market. We could have some of that while we wait for traffic to calm down," I said.

Maybe if I were worried about karma, I'd have tried harder to mend the rupture before our guests left respectively angry and disappointed. But I didn't have any expectation that I'd be able to change Mike's perspective on the concept of gender identity, certainly not in a single evening after many beers. And like Mike, I don't believe in all that woo-woo stuff, in karma.

"I'm just tired," Jaime said tensely, already standing.

We clumped ourselves in the hall while our guests put on their things, and I waved to Amy as she walked beside Jaime down the breezeway to the stairs.

Mike stood behind me as we watched them go and massaged my shoulders. I could hear the sound his thumbs made against the cloth of my shirt, a soft scratching hush. And though I strained to hear something more, the coalescing human noises of the whole world from beyond the apartment, all I could hear was Mike. His thumbs, his stomach, his pulse, all that kept him alive behind me.

* * *

This story first appeared in the After Dinner Conversation—April 2023 issue.

Discussion Questions

1. The first half of the story discusses reincarnation. Do you believe in reincarnation or a form of reincarnation? If so, what (*if anything*) is the purpose of reincarnation?
2. The story also talks about soulmates. Do you believe in soulmates or some variation of soulmates?
3. The third part of the story talks about sexual orientation, gender identity, and gender fluidity. Do you believe that sometimes people are born the wrong gender or that people can be both gay and born the wrong gender (*i.e., a gay man that was born into a woman's body*)?
4. In the cases of questions 1, 2, and 3, what are the scientific, religious, experiential, or value-based constructs we overlay that cause us to come to our own conclusions for each question?
5. In the story, Jaime was born a biological woman, transitioned to a man, but is going to have a baby. Mike questions how to define a man (*or a woman?*) if not by the ability to have children. What would be your answer to this question?

* * *

The Draft

Jan McCleery

* * *

Throngs of people entered the fifteen-story building crowned by the gold sign reading, *Center for the RTL Headquarters*. Most had no idea what *RTL* stood for.

Valets were running back and forth in front of the building, taking the next expensive car in the long line that circled the block before entering the curved driveway. Men in tuxedos and women in cocktail dresses emerged from their cars. Servers passed out champagne to those in the long line waiting to enter the building. Once inside, they entered a massive conference room with huge screens on several walls displaying the words *Center for the RTL*. A live five-piece orchestra played chamber music. Servers with trays of upscale appetizers circulated the room as the attendees milled about, greeting business associates. Empty champagne glasses were promptly replaced.

Congressman Mitch Mitchell and his wife, Gloria, were a handsome couple in their early fifties. Mitch had been swept into his seat in Congress in the 2022 midterms when he was only thirty, running on a strict pro-life platform. As they stood talking to a billionaire contributor and his wife, the lights dimmed. A deep male voice reverberated from above: "Welcome to the grand opening of the Center for the RTL. Now... here is the Founder and CEO, Dr. Celeste Rivers."

A trim woman with intelligent green eyes and short dark hair framing her pixie face eagerly took the stage and walked into the spotlight. The screens around the room projected her image. Smiling. Beaming. Charismatic. She doubted anyone knew she was thinking about how needing a hysterectomy all those years ago in college had been such an unexpected blessing, leaving her free to pursue a Stanford PhD in engineering and accomplish what had become her life's goal: to give all women in America a choice whether or not to bear a child. Now it had become a reality. Her heart beat in her chest with a combination of pride and excitement.

"Thank you all for coming," she said, her voice strong and clear. "What you will see and hear today will amaze and thrill you. It is the beginning of an era of new freedom for all women! The letters R-T-L stand for 'Right to Life.' As of today, all women can embrace the right to life without relinquishing the right to control their bodies."

The women involved with the project for the past ten years started applauding wildly. Others clapped politely but looked confused.

Celeste continued, "Today, we have the technology to allow a fetus to grow safely and healthily, from embryo to a fully developed newborn, without using a woman's body." She paused. "Behold, the incubators."

The screens displayed pictures of the center's incubation rooms. Dimly lit, each room was filled with hundreds and hundreds of incubators: some pods contained small fetuses with enlarged heads and small limbs curled into a C-shape; others held nearly full-grown babies. It was like an eerie scene from a science fiction movie.

The mood in the conference room quickly changed; some gasped. Celeste was prepared, and the screens quickly changed to a series of beautiful babies wrapped in blankets and held by their beaming mothers.

"Babies who are gestated in our incubators are healthier. No more preemies born too early due to their mother's medical issues. No more crack babies or those addicted to alcohol. Healthy babies who will bond with their mothers. Gretchen, model your baby cord for us, please."

A beautiful, tall, young, Germanic woman, all in red from her hair to her luscious lips and down to her bikini and spiky heels, mounted the stairs to join Celeste on the stage, towering over her. Low on her waist hung a gossamer silky string.

"What is that I see you wearing?" Celeste asked mischievously.

"My red bikini?" Gretchen answered her rehearsed line, spoken with a heavy German accent while flashing a smile.

Celeste winked at the audience. "She knows." People laughed, men nervously because they couldn't help staring at the striking woman on the stage.

"You mean this?" Gretchen pointed to the gossamer string. "It's my 'baby cord.' It's letting me feel what my baby is doing, just as if he was right here in my tummy." She patted her flat, bare stomach.

"Do you mind if a few of our guests feel what you do?"

"I don't mind. My husband is fascinated by it."

Celeste motioned to the audience. "Come toward the stage." She didn't need to urge. Men were pushing to get forward. Gretchen knelt, and Celeste leaned down and held a mic as the stunning woman let a few people take turns placing their hands on her stomach.

Every monitor had gone to split screen, half showing the beautiful Gretchen letting men feel her bare stomach; the other half displayed an image of her baby in the incubator, kicking and squirming.

In turn, each exclaimed, "Wow!" "I felt it kick!" "That's amazing!"

Celeste laughed. "Thank you, Gretchen."

The tall redhead stood, smiled sweetly at the men, and left the stage.

"We've placed one thousand RTL Clinics at prior Planned Parenthood sites plus added hundreds more in rural areas. Any woman can easily get to one of our clinics, where her fetus will be removed and whisked to the nearest center to be placed in an incubator. Near the end of term, the mother will be notified and given an appointment date."

On the screens, a swaddled baby is taken to a seated mother, who immediately puts her newborn to her breast to nurse. Her husband sits by her side, his arm lovingly around her. In the next view, the couple stands up with their baby, is handed a "New Baby Gift Bag," and walks out the front door.

Celeste added, "Better than the stork!"

Laughter and excitement filled the room.

"Now, are there any questions?"

A woman reporter was the first to raise her hand. When Celeste pointed to her, she pushed her horn-rimmed glasses further up her nose. "Judith Baker, *Today's Times Magazine.*" She pursed her thin lips. "Are you playing God here?"

Everyone quieted. A few gasped at the implications.

"Believe me," Celeste responded, "we wrestled with difficult questions. Think of it. We could eliminate babies with gene defects. Alter survival rates based on sex, race, or other traits. Create a master race." Her voice had gotten louder as she raised her eyebrows, a look she knew made her appear sinister, and she looked around the audience. Not everyone was smiling. In fact, some looked shocked.

"But that would be playing God, wouldn't it?" Celeste chastised. "That would be altering the natural balance and plan. We said 'No!' Rest assured. We are not playing God. We are providing an alternate womb for women. Plain and simple."

Some people nodded approvingly. Celeste pointed at another reporter.

"Annie Walker, *World News,*" the woman said. "What if the mother didn't want a baby?"

"Good question. After her fetus is extracted, she has up until the time of full gestation to decide whether, at the end, she wants to claim the baby or put it up for adoption. Same as the current US law. Next?"

A male reporter raised his hand. "Gerald Cross, ALT Cable News," he opened. "Won't this result in significantly more babies born per year? We all know many women buy smuggled contraceptives and abortion pills, and there are ways for women to obtain illegal abortions. Now women and their doctors will have no reason to take that risk. Won't we end up with millions of babies without mothers?"

Celeste shrugged her shoulders and didn't answer.

Gerald countered, "But what's the plan? Won't all these extra babies overwhelm the system?"

Celeste smiled sweetly. "That's an excellent question. Why don't you answer it for us? For the past few decades, the political party your station supports has pushed for every fertilized egg to result in a baby. They have outlawed contraception and all abortions. So, if there is now a problem of too many babies, it is up to your party to solve it. Next question?" And with that, she looked away from Gerald.

* * *

The Women's Revolution

Soon, all women were taking advantage of the free service. The gossamer strings became a sign of motherhood, like a rounded, protruding belly had in years past. No longer having to deal with stretch marks and bulging stomachs, expectant mothers wore bikinis at the beach to show off their baby cords.

Released from the need to use their bodies to grow babies, women used their newfound freedom to pursue higher education, and the number of women in better-paying jobs increased. More women entered the government and formed a new political party, "The Women's Right to Life" party, and soon women were in control of the country: Congress, the White House, and most state governments.

As Gerald from ALT News had predicted, before long, the availability of babies had overwhelmed adoption agencies and foster system.

The government created the "Office of Equality and Fairness" (OEF) to resolve the problem and established "The

Draft" system. According to Draft rules, all males between the ages of sixteen and fifty must be entered into a lottery to determine which among them would, under penalty of law, take the unclaimed babies.

Of course, men fought back, whining it wasn't fair to select only males to take unwanted babies. The OEF's answer came first in the form of questions: Who, for centuries, were forced to subject their bodies to the strain of growing unwanted babies? And who were often left to raise those children with no support from anyone, no matter how many children they already had? Who had to leave school—sometimes as young as sixteen years of age—and despair of ever being able to secure a better future? The answer: Women. "Well," the OEF argued, "now is the time for men to step up, take their turn, and accept responsibility."

The Draft Rules were solidified, and men realized the law would not be changed, not in the near future.

On January 13, 2050, "The Draft" went into effect.

* * *

January 13, 2067

Tim Mitchell woke up when four-year-old Curt jumped on him and pummeled him in the face. Tim grabbed Curt's hands and held him firmly, trying to quiet his aggression.

The sun was barely up. Having reached the age of fifty, Tim knew this was his last year; after this, he would no longer be eligible for the Draft. He had ducked it for the first sixteen years after it was established, but for the last four years in a row, he had been a big loser and was now raising four children under the age of five.

Curt, his first child, was born with a rare genetic disability that left him with cognitive learning problems as well as anger issues. He barely spoke and still had to be spoon-fed and diapered. Tim had to quit his job to raise Curt.

When Curt was diagnosed, Tim's fury was directed at his father, former Congressman Mitch Mitchell, who had been a fervent advocate to end all forms of birth control and abortion.

Tim had called his father and screamed, "What were you guys thinking? What did you imagine would happen if abortions and contraception were outlawed?" But Tim knew his father was tired of being blamed. Tim's mother still blamed Mitch for Lizzy's death. Tim's sister had committed suicide when she found herself pregnant in college. She was Congressman Mitchell's daughter, and abortion was not an option. Now Mitch's son had joined the blame game. Mitch hung up on him.

Max and Lucy, ages two and three, heard the commotion and padded into Tim's bedroom in their one-piece PJs. Tim carried screaming Curt into the kitchen. Max and Lucy followed him. Tim left Roger, less than one year old, in his crib.

The three were eating their cereal—well Max and Lucy were, Curt was throwing his—but Tim couldn't wait any longer. He turned on the TV. He'd missed the standard opening, the pomp and ceremony, but it was always the same.

The President greets the emcee, who comes on stage with a great deal of fanfare, clapping, and music. "Elmer Greco," the President says, smiling. "Are we ready for this year's excitement?"

Elmer is a flamboyant man. His hair is waved up too high in front, and his white teeth gleam. He's got on too much makeup, even by TV standards.

When Tim turned on the TV this year, Elmer was seated by the large wheel, beaming. Tim checked the board for his best friend George's birthday, May 17th. Number 279. "Lucky bastard," Tim muttered under his breath. "He's ducked it again." Tim and George had worked together at the ad agency until Tim's first unlucky draw. Men with numbers higher than two hundred rarely ended up with a baby at their doorstep.

Tim's birthday, July 19th, had not yet been called.

Now Elmer spun for July 15th. "The lucky number is..." The huge roulette wheel spun, click-clack-click, then stopped at 330.

"Aw, 330!" exclaimed Elmer, disappointed. "That's a high number. Better luck next year."

It annoyed Tim to no end that a high number could be bad. That everyone could be so cheery, so upbeat about low numbers. Changing men's lives forever. It was atrocious!

Curt's yelling distracted Tim for a moment. Then Elmer called out, "July 19th." Tim stared at the TV, shaking.

Time stopped. The world slowed down as the wheel clicked, making its way around the large circle. Then it decelerated. All motion stopped. Everything around Tim stopped. The kids stopped yelling. Roger in his crib stopped crying. There was nothing. Nothing. Except... the number... "5."

His heart sank. It couldn't be! "Five! *Five?*"

Tim could barely function. He picked up the phone. "Cindy! Can you come over and cover me here?"

"Sure, Tim." His next-door neighbor was compassionate. She, too, had been watching the Draft, worrying about Tim, fearing he couldn't handle yet another child. She knew he was already on the edge.

Through his mind fog, Tim grabbed a warm coat, put it over his pajamas, and rushed out in his slippers as Cindy came in, facing four screaming kids.

Tim exited the apartment building into the chill of the morning. Standing in the street, he didn't hear a taxi honking as it roared by. "Just run me over," Tim muttered. The next cab stopped, and he jumped in. He gave the driver the address for the agency he'd worked for until the unlucky year when he'd lost the Draft for the first time.

He jumped out of the cab, ran into the building, and took the elevator to the tenth floor. He walked right by Millie, the receptionist.

"Tim? Tim. You can't go in there."

He ignored her and burst into George's office. George, who had never lost the Draft, looked up from his desk. Lucky bastard.

"Did you see? Did you see?" Tim stammered.

"The Draft? I watched until they called my number, then got a phone call and had to get to work. Lucky, huh?" Suddenly, George seemed to become aware of Tim's expression. "Oh... my... God, Tim. What number did you get?"

"Five! Five! I fucking got five! I'm dead, man. I can't do it. I've got Curt driving me crazy. Roger's still in his crib. Number five? Why is there no sense to it? No limits? I called the Center last year after they dropped Roger on my doorstep and screamed at them. 'How can you do this to me?' Do you know what they said? 'Men made the laws that said all fertilized eggs must become babies. These are your rules.'"

"They aren't *my* rules," sobbed Tim. "They're my dad's rules. Not *my* rules."

George looked at Tim with anguish but had no words. All men were powerless in America now.

* * *

February 28, 2067

On February 28, it happened. There was a knock on Tim's door. He felt dread, not expecting any visitors except one, the Center for the RTL.

He opened the door reluctantly. A woman stood in the hallway, smiling, accompanied by two others, each holding a bundle.

"You're so lucky! You've got twins!"

Six weeks later, Tim was exhausted. The way he'd been every day since Curt arrived. But he was more than exhausted: drained, shattered, incoherent. He'd spent another day trying to rock the twins and get them to eat. Curt screamed at the top of his lungs. Lucy and Max demanded attention. Roger, Curt, and Max still in diapers in addition to the twins. Finally, Lucy, Max, and Roger were in their beds.

Tim watched the twins, asleep in his arms. He couldn't believe how beautiful they were. It made him so sad. Holding one in each arm, he tiptoed into the bedroom to check that Lucy and Max were asleep. He smiled at Lucy's sweet face, at Max's cuteness. As he entered the babies' room, Roger was asleep in his crib, but when the floor creaked, he awoke. Now all three were crying.

He put the twins down, then went from one crib to the other, trying to soothe them, rubbing their backs. They were still fussing, but Tim, completely beat, left and shut the door to the room, ignoring their cries. Curt was watching TV. Tim knew the boy would either crash in front of the TV for the night or scream around midnight for his dad to get up and take him into their bed. Curt had never been able to sleep in a bed alone.

Tim crept by softly so as not to attract Curt's attention, unlocked the front door, and then headed quietly to the bathroom. He shut the door and telephoned Cindy. "I need your help."

"Sorry, Tim, but it's late. Maybe tomorrow."

"No," he said it quietly, but even he could hear the despair in his tone. "The kids need your help... now. Tomorrow will be too late."

"What's wrong, Tim?"

But Tim couldn't answer. He had slashed his wrists and was bleeding to death on the bathroom floor.

* * *

Becoming a Grandparent

"Mr. Mitchell?" the policeman on the porch asked.

"Yes?" Mitch Mitchell felt a sense of dread; whatever it was, he knew it wasn't going to be good.

"We are sorry to inform you that your son, Tim, passed away last night."

Mitch was stunned, but he remained stoic. "How?"

"I'm sorry, sir. He committed suicide."

Mitch just stood, shocked. They hadn't been close since Tim drew his first unlucky number in the Draft. His wife, Gloria, had passed away a year after Tim first lost the Draft. She'd never gotten over blaming Mitch for Lizzy's death. Then seeing Tim with a problem child had broken her heart.

Mitch didn't know what to feel. He simply thanked the policeman, who turned and left.

As soon as he was alone, Mitch's phone rang.

"Mr. Mitchell?"

"Yes."

"This is Director Martin from the Center for the Right to Life." The woman's authoritative voice was irritating. "Don't go anywhere. We have paperwork we need you to sign."

"What's this about?"

"Please don't leave, sir. That would cause you legal difficulty. We will be right there."

Click.

Ten minutes later, when he responded to the knock on his door, he saw two black cars parked in front of his Maryland residence. A tall woman with a "Center for the RTL" patch stood on his porch. Mitch looked at her warily. Her nametag said, *Martin.*

"This shouldn't take long, sir. Is there a place we can sit down and review the paperwork?"

"What paperwork?"

"Please, sir, the explanation is in the paperwork. Where can we sit and review it?"

He motioned her to sit on the couch, and he took a chair.

She sat, put her binder down on the coffee table between them, and opened it to the first page.

Mitchell Adoption, it read in large bold letters. Suddenly realizing the implications, Mitch felt his eyes grow wide. "I can't... what? What is this?"

"Obviously, sir, your son's unfortunate demise means he can no longer fulfill his obligations to the government to care for his six children."

"Six?" Mitch stammered, then he remembered about the twins.

"Since Tim never legally assigned a godparent, the responsibility falls to you, his father, the children's grandfather."

"No, what? I'm seventy-five years old. I can't take on six children, twin babies."

"Legally, they are your responsibility."

"Take them back to the Center!" he directed.

"That wouldn't be legal," Director Martin answered coldly. She paused, and her voice softened a bit. "I understand this is happening suddenly, but there are no other options. The responsibility is yours and yours alone."

She turned to the signature page in the binder and held out a pen. "Sign," she directed. He looked at the doorway and saw two guards, armed, standing there at attention. He understood. *Take the children or go to jail.* He signed.

She rose and left six folders on the coffee table, each labeled with one of the children's names. The last name on each was Mitchell. "I am sure you will be a good grandparent to the children. But, of course, there are significant fines and legal issues for men who shirk their duty. Oh, and I suggest you identify a godparent. You're getting up there in age." He could see a slight smirk on her face. Then her face softened. "We will bring the children in now. Please greet them warmly. They have been through a lot."

She turned and went to the door. Mitch sat, shocked. He couldn't think straight. Then Lucy and Max ran in with tears in their eyes and hugged him. "Oh, Grandpa. Daddy's gone," little Lucy sobbed. They had only seen their grandfather a few times at Christmas, but they remembered him. Kids do.

Curt walked up and kicked him in the shin.

The children's clothes, toys, diapers, a week's supply of food and formula, and multiple car seats were carried in and set down on the floor. Finally, the twins came, pushed in a double baby carriage.

"This is Inge," Director Martin introduced the tall, gray-haired, Swedish woman, helping Roger toddle in. "She will assist you in making a smooth transition with the children today. It's a new service we offer for the children's sake. She can lend a hand as you prepare lists of how to care and feed them and make school plans. She can stay until the children are in bed tonight and can return during the day tomorrow if you still need her and then offer phone consultations for a week."

He nodded, relieved that he wasn't going to just suddenly be left with them all. "Yes, please."

Inge held Max's and Lucy's hands while Mitch carried a squirming Curt and showed the children their rooms. A staff member set up two cribs, and another staffer carried Roger to one of them and then went back for the twins. Inge began moving their belongings into their rooms.

Director Martin said, "Could I have one more word with you, sir? Alone."

Inge picked up Curt and carried him into the den where Max and Lucy were watching TV, leaving only Director Martin and Mitch in the living room.

"You know, during your time as Congressman, women didn't *want* to make the choice between bearing an unwanted child or having an abortion. Young girls still in high school, women who were raped or with too many children already, women just feeling they had no control over their bodies and their lives. I think men in America now understand how the loss of control feels when the government makes the decisions about your life. I really hope this will work out for you and your grandchildren. They need you. And I am sorry for your loss, sir."

She left and shut the door softly behind her. A tear rolled down his cheek.

* * *

This story first appeared in the After Dinner Conversation—May 2023 issue.

Discussion Questions

1. What do you think would happen if women could easily and cheaply have a newly conceived child removed and grown outside of their body? How do you think society would change?

2. Would you support a law that required men to have a 50/50 chance of being the primary caregiver for the children of all unplanned pregnancies?

3. Assuming there were far more children placed in adoption than those looking to adopt, would you support a "Draft" like the one in the story? Why or why not? Do you have an alternative?

4. Given the choice between easy and inexpensive access to incubated babies, like in the story, and easy and inexpensive access to contraception and abortion, which would you prefer and why?

5. Does the government have a responsibility to provide excellent care for unwanted children? What societal advantages/disadvantages exist in pushing that responsibility onto individuals through a system like the story's "Draft"?

* * *

The Human Experience

Jared Cappel

* * *

Always make them wait. Couples love to talk, young ones especially. We're not allowed to record them, but there are no laws on amplifying. Our waiting area is designed to project their voices, magnifying their speech and feeding it directly into my earpiece.

It's important to get a good look at them too. The wife, Morgan, is clearly on edge. She walks around the room, studying every fold in the wall, like a dog sniffing around the perimeter of her yard. Her husband, Thad, sinks into a chair, a pile of pamphlets in his hands. He flips through them, rolling his eyes, tossing them aside. One final pamphlet catches his eye—a list of packages with a detailed breakdown. This wasn't on the website.

Morgan seems nervous; Thad, angry. This is important to know. Morgan controls their general discourse, but Thad likely has the final say. His tone is rather gruff, insisting. When he speaks, his wife listens. When she speaks, which is often, he barely acknowledges her, refusing to lift his eyes from the pamphlets.

I make them wait another ten minutes before letting them into my office. I've gathered all the intel I'm likely to obtain, but the longer they wait, the more the power shifts into my hand. A simple tactic, and a rather understated one at that, but it's effective. We have the data to prove it.

The couple is much friendlier to me than they were to each other. They shake my hand, accept some coffee, settle into the chairs across the desk from mine. Morgan begins rambling off all the information she's learned about our process. Some of the statements are posed as questions but, really, she's just trying to impress how much she knows. It's clear she's read a lot into this. I rate her understanding of our procedures in the upper range.

Thad is still focused on the pamphlet in his hand. The details in the pamphlet are a bit different than on the website. This is intentional, though there's no way for him to know that. He becomes rather specific and accusatory with his questions. His voice remains gruff; his words, deservedly paranoid. His understanding of our procedures isn't quite to the level of his wife's, but his distrusting nature is rather astute.

I smile to let them know their concerns are heard, and I pull a form from the second drawer of my desk. "Before we get into all that, have you decided which package you are thinking of purchasing?"

"The gold," Morgan says, "though we'd consider the platinum if you can talk us into it."

"Honey, we discussed this." Thad hands me a stack of papers. "We qualified for a loan for the gold package. We really can't afford anything higher."

I give the documents a perfunctory glance and begin to fill out some information on my form. "This all appears in order. We do have other financing options available for the platinum package, but we'll get to that in good time."

Morgan leans forward in her chair, lowers her voice to a whisper. "Is it really true that the platinum package is the highest?"

"Yes. It's been written into law."

"Well yeah, we know that, but surely royalty and such aren't locked into such restrictions like us plebeians."

"I can assure you they are."

"I don't believe it."

Thad nudges his wife and signals for her to be quiet. "She's just an employee, dear. If there's anything shady going on, she wouldn't know the half of it." He smiles at me. "No offense, of course."

There's nothing he can say that would really offend me, but his assumption of my naïveté certainly works in my favor. Any issues he raises can be deflected to the company. "None taken," I say, "but I am quite confident no one can go above platinum. The entire process is codified, made public, and reviewed for irregularities."

"We've read the website," Morgan says, then stops herself. "Sorry, you must take me for quite the shrew."

"It's okay. All hopeful parents just want what's best."

"Or second best in our case," Thad says with a smile, but his wife isn't laughing. He continues. "Please tell us more about the gold package."

"The gold package entitles you to one hundred and fifty additional attribute points, which you can give to your unborn child across any or all of the eight domains—physical health, mental health, attractiveness, intelligence, likability, athleticism, confidence, and our newest attribute luck."

"Luck?"

"Yes, if you place your points on luck, the attributes will be spread at random across the domains."

Morgan laughs. "Can you imagine that, honey? Leaving all this to chance... like barbarians!"

Thad doesn't quite catch his wife's comment, his attention lost deep in the folds of the pamphlet with the divergent information. "It says here with the gold package, we start with fifty points in each domain?"

"Not quite," I explain. "You get fifty points for both physical and mental health, meaning your child will be born with average genetic makeup in these domains. In the other domains, your child starts out at twenty-five, meaning they're at the twenty-fifth percentile."

"So below average."

"Yes, in a sense, but you have one hundred and fifty other points to play with. If you want to do things conservatively, you could spread the points evenly across the six lower domains, and your child's genes will be perfectly average."

"Average?" Thad asks. "This is an awfully expensive way to end up with an average child, don't you think? Seems like mother nature could do that herself."

"But can she guarantee it?"

Thad slinks back into his chair and stuffs the pamphlet into the breast pocket of his jacket.

"Or you can place the points on the attributes that are most important to you," I say.

"What attributes do most parents go for?" Morgan asks.

"For many years, physical health was our top seller, but it's since been passed by mental health. Many parents realize there's not much to life without happiness."

"So our child can be happy as long as it's ugly and dimwitted?"

I summon a line from my script. "I really think you're underscoring just how many points you have to play with. Why don't you use the attribute bars on the monitors to see how much freedom you really have?"

I swivel two monitors in front of the hopeful young parents-to-be. They each take their own approach to building the perfect child. Thad focuses on intelligence, athleticism, and health, jacking up the points in these attributes at the expense of the others. Morgan is more conservative with her choices, trying to make sure her prospective child doesn't lag in any one area.

Morgan scowls at her husband. "So you want a child with no confidence?"

"It'll be confident because of how damn capable it is."

"Uh-huh, all people with a 28-likability score are brimming with confidence. People love to be loathed."

"Well, at least the child I created can use its intelligence to excel. What is your average Jane going to accomplish in life? You need talents to get ahead. You can't get anywhere sludging through the middle."

"My child will be healthy, intelligent, and reasonably capable. What more can we ask for?"

"Greatness!"

The couple is getting a bit agitated, and I use this to my advantage. "Greatness comes at a price, I'm afraid. If the limited number of points doesn't suffice, you can always consider an upgrade to our platinum package."

Thad's voice comes back gruff. "We already told you, it's out of our price range."

"Yes, I understand. However, you can take out a loan in your unborn child's name to pay for the upgrade."

"You want us to indebt our unborn child?"

"Forget unborn, the poor child has yet to be conceived!"

"Don't think of it as a loan," I say, another line from my script. "Think of it as an opportunity. With the advantages this will give the child in life, the loan should be easily paid in full by age thirty, and once paid off, the child will maintain all of the increased attributes."

"Should be?"

"Yes, there's still the randomness of the human experience, you understand. We only provide a genetic guarantee, but how those genes are expressed must be left to mother nature, as per international law. Not to worry, though, good genes invariably lead to good people. Our repayment rate is over 85 percent."

"And the other 15 percent?"

"Typically, that's from parents who don't spread the attributes wisely. We've since introduced stricter measures for our platinum package, and we expect that number to drop in the upcoming years."

Morgan leans in, drops her voice to a whisper. "I have one last question for you."

I laugh. Even if I hadn't eavesdropped on them in the waiting room, I'd be well aware of what she's going to ask. "Let me guess, sub-domains?"

The young couple's eyes light up.

"I'm afraid those violate international law."

"You really want us to believe that if some billionaire walked in, he couldn't pay to have his child's height altered?"

"If height were said billionaire's paramount goal, he could raise the attributes of domains he felt might affect height, such as attractiveness or athleticism. But there's no way to select for such specific human qualities."

"Why? I mean, I know it's the law, but nobody's ever been able to clearly explain why."

I know exactly why, but I play the part of the naïve office worker and echo the company line. "From what I understand, it's the same reason we can't offer a package above platinum. If humans were given the choice, they'd crank all attributes to one hundred. When everyone's at one hundred, nobody's at one hundred. We need these rules to maintain the human experience."

The young couple look at each other, whisper a few things into each other's ears. The amplification works well. They think I'm lying; of course, they do. I am. I hate when couples bring up the sub-domains, a topic I can discuss but not deliver upon. I need to redirect to the packages we do have, to the deals I can close. "The platinum package comes with an additional hundred points, allowing you to create a child that is well above average and poised for a successful life."

Thad won't admit it, but he's intrigued. "Remind me how much more the platinum package costs."

"Double the price of our gold package."

"Wait, double?" Morgan cuts in. "I read it was only a 50 percent increase."

"Yes, that's true, but that's for parents who are able to pay our price up front. Due to the risk of loaning to an unborn child, our fees do go up considerably."

The room falls silent as the young couple tries to process all the information being thrown at them. It's important for me to step out mid-meeting, to get an accurate sense of what the couple is really thinking, and now seems to be as good of a time as any. I get to my feet. "I can tell I've given you a lot to discuss. I'm going to run to the bathroom and give you a chance to think more about this decision. If you need anything, just open the door and holler."

I leave the room and peer through a strategically placed eyehole which gives me a full view of my office. My earpiece continues to relay what is being said.

Morgan turns to her husband. "What do you think about all this?"

He motions for her to be quiet. He reaches into a briefcase and produces a small handheld device resembling a ray gun. This is certainly an interesting development. He walks briskly throughout the room, aiming the gun at different surfaces. He sweeps the room with expert precision; it's clear he's been trained well.

"What on earth are you doing?" his wife asks. "What is that?"

"Quiet. Just give me a second." The gun emits a powerful ray that appears red to the human eye. He aims it at the walls, at my phone, at the underside of my desk, all the while saying, "Test." He's waiting for something to reflect back green. There's only one thing in that office that will come back green. I wonder if he'll find it.

His search comes back empty. He turns to his wife, speaking in a whisper. "It's illegal for them to record us. There's nothing to stop them from amplifying our voices, though. I wanted to make sure they aren't listening."

"Are they?"

"Not that I can tell."

"How do you know all this?"

"I just do." His voice is particularly insistent, and she lets the matter drop. "So what do you think?"

"It could be a good idea."

"I don't know, sounds like a scam to me. How would you feel if your parents took out a loan for you before you were even born?"

"How would you feel if your parents didn't give you every possible chance to thrive?"

"It just seems expensive, is all. What's the point of a great life if you spend the whole thing buried in debt?"

The questions are rather typical. I'm not really learning much that I didn't already know. The only real development is the presence of the ray gun. He's slid it back into his briefcase. I need to find a way for him to pull it out again. I press a button on my handheld device, which emits a staticky sound into the office. We use this when we want couples to feel they're being watched.

He takes the bait. He reaches for the gun and begins to sweep the room once more. He lifts my phone and scans the underside. I quickly reenter.

"I wish you'd put that down," I say, maintaining a professional voice.

He lets the phone slide from his fingers, tries to conceal

the item in his hand.

"We're not recording you if that's your fear," I say. "That would be highly illegal."

"No, it's not that..."

"We're not listening either."

He looks bashful. It's the first time all day I've seen an honest emotion out of him. The tough veneer has finally cracked; some humanity oozes out.

"I didn't think ordinary citizens were permitted the use of sound wave detectors," I say.

His eyes bulge. Another honest reaction. This time he's at a loss for words.

I reach for the form I had started to fill out earlier. "It says here that you work in construction."

"Well, yes, technically..."

"Technically?" his wife asks.

"Sound wave detectors are only permitted to those with government clearance," I say. "If we're going to process your loan, we need you to be honest with us."

"He's in construction," Morgan says. "Right, honey?"

Thad shifts in his seat. "Right." His voice lacks conviction.

"Mm-hmm," I say. "Except that's not exactly true, is it?"

Thad looks sheepishly at his wife, says nothing.

This is the chance I've been waiting for; one I rarely get. "Due to the inaccurate information provided in your loan documents, we won't be able to proceed with the gold package. However, as the loan for the platinum package would be in your child's name, we could still proceed. Please note, however, that this decision would have to be made today. Should you leave our office without a deal, I will have to file a report on your inaccurate loan documents that will invalidate you from further using our services."

"I don't understand," Morgan says.

"I think your husband does," I say. "I could step outside again if you'd like."

Thad says nothing but nods.

I reenter the waiting room with a newfound sense of interest. These meetings tend to go the same way; the presence of the sound wave detector has changed everything. I wonder if he buys my threat.

"They're listening to us, I'm sure of it," Thad says.

"How can you be so sure?"

"How can she know about sound wave detectors? She could only know if she had seen one herself."

"How can *she* know? How can *you* know?"

He stares down his wife, urges her to let the matter drop.

"If you don't trust them, we can go somewhere else," Morgan says.

"There's no point. Once they enter into the system that we used false loan documents, we'll be flagged everywhere. I think we better just go through with this. I can't be flagged. My boss will find out."

I can hardly believe my ears. He's doing my work for me.

"I'm just worried about the loan," Morgan says. "What if our child never pays it off?"

"We can account for that." Thad reaches to the monitor and begins to adjust the attribute bars, paying particular attention to measures like intelligence. The young couple argues back and forth. The confidence they had arrived with is long gone, replaced with a foreboding sense that any decision they make (or don't make) will doom their unborn offspring.

Morgan begins to fiddle around with her monitor, too, using the additional one hundred attribute points to build the perfect child who could fare well in the most important measures while retaining a sense of balance. Her apprehension begins to fade as she sees the ever-increasing scores.

Thad gets to his feet, opens the door, asks me to return. My eyes fall to the monitors in front of the couple. "Wow, both of your proposed children look rather similar!"

"They do, don't they?"

"It's the best of both worlds," I say, a line from my script. "The security of a healthy child, with the promise of an exceptional one. So, should we finish filling out that paperwork?"

It takes another fifteen minutes to fill out the form and explain the genetic testing and conception process that will take place. Thad stays uncharacteristically quiet. Morgan badgers me with questions that I am easily able to answer. When we're finished with the forms, I shake their hands and walk them to the door. "Remember, if you have any more questions, you should find all the answers on the pamphlet." I tap the pamphlet in Thad's breast pocket.

The young couple thanks me for my hard work and exits. They seem nervous but excited, as all new parents should be. I wait until they get into their car and drive off, and then I pull out my own sound wave detector and aim it around the room. "Test, test," I repeat. Most of the waiting room glows a faint shade of green, as expected, as the room has been built to amplify sound.

When I aim the sound wave detector at the stack of

pamphlets, they reflect a vibrant shade of green, a fitting color really, the color of money, the color of my money now that I've sold another platinum package.

* * *

This story first appeared in the After Dinner Conversation—February 2021 issue.

"The Human Experience" also previously appeared in Jared Cappel's short story collection of the same name.

Discussion Questions

1. Which, if any, of the things that take place in the story do you find the most immoral and/or disturbing and why?

2. If the technology was available to change the attributes of your child for a price, would you do it? If so, what attributes would you focus on and why?

3. Is it immoral to incur debt that continues on to the child if it goes unpaid by the parent? Does it matter that the debt is for a purchase that will potentially help the child's future?

4. If you could find out how you genetically rated on various attributes compared to the general population, would you want to know? If yes, what attributes would you want to know about and why?

5. What, if any, difference is there between a wealthy parent that is able to stay home, play with their child, and provide their child with mental stimulation so the child has the best chance at a good future versus the parents in the story who have the money to do this genetically? In both cases, aren't wealthy parents simply using their money to help secure their child's future?

* * *

The Crate

David Rich

* * *

I cruised out of BLE's house in my crate. A teenaged girl like myself, she was one of the few people I'd ever seen in person.

I stopped my crate in no place in particular to flat out break the law. I was so good at hacking crates that I'd reprogrammed mine to open upon command. Crazy illegal!

All crates were programmed to protect everyone's fundamental right not to be seen. Basically, they remained closed until confirming you're in the presence of only legally sanctioned live contacts. Then you go back in before seeing any unauthorized people.

History recounts that long ago, people judged one another by things such as gender, ethnicity, occupation, personal transportation vehicle, etc. But the modern American Political Union, our beloved A.P.U., made that intrinsically impossible.

When the door opened, I stepped out of my crate into

broad daylight. Although my actions were illicit, I expected no witnesses and deemed them as harmless.

I viewed a sea of crates, perfectly identical boxes on wheels, rolling to their individual destinations. Inside each, I imagined a human being enjoying physical isolation by texting, gaming, taking in media, or any number of things.

Then, I glimpsed a mother and child crossing the street. I believe they were of Asian descent (though we rarely spoke of ethnic physical traits). Certainly, they'd legally arranged to walk wherever they were headed. But we weren't supposed to see one another.

The girl stared at me; she didn't appear old enough to understand the law. When the mother spotted me, she made her daughter look away and hurried her along.

The moment was amazing. They were two random people I'd never seen before. Above all, I'd beaten the system. I was powerful. The mother who'd seen me couldn't disguise her horror.

It was exhilarating.

* * *

Of the people I'd known in person, all but BLE were family relations. BLE was my only "live" friend; all my remaining friends were still virtual. It was a sore subject for me. I suspect that by my age, most had several legally sanctioned live friends.

I remembered hacking BLE's crate profile and learning that she had six live friends and many more virtual friends than I did. Knowing things like that was forbidden because comparisons can make people feel inferior. And in this case, I was angry! It'd made no sense to me that she'd have more friends.

I knew I was much smarter than BLE and made frequent hints about it without telling her explicitly. I couldn't risk that she'd lodge a complaint, or worse, record the conversation.

If you denigrated anyone, they caught you. If you compared and contrasted people's merits and flaws, they caught you.

I'd been accused of revealing my own accomplishments from time to time. Usually, the AI's caught it in my text messages. Fortunately, minor correct speech violations resulted in either warnings or assignments to watch dreadful reeducation videos.

One had to be subtle. So, earlier that afternoon, I'd managed a casual comment regarding the ease of last week's chemistry exam. Her riled glance was priceless.

Despite our complicated relationship, we were indispensable allies in solving a mutual problem.

We both wanted to flee the American Political Union.

It seemed obvious why I'd want to leave. How infuriating it had been, possessing superior intelligence, to be considered merely an equal in a sea of perfectly identical crates!

But BLE?

I knew she was distinctively pleasant and engaging in person, though I had minimal data to compare. Perhaps I'd always suspected she didn't belong hidden in a crate.

The hare came through, BLE texted. In our secret code, that meant one of her many friendship connections had provided the geographic coordinates of a gap in the electronic border fence confining the A.P.U.'s population.

About a thousand rabbit holes, she continued texting. That meant the ride to the gap was a thousand kilometers. A long way! But I'd successfully mastered how to disable our crates' travel limiters and location transmitters without losing auto-navigation. The next steps simply were to choose a day and cover story, empty our currency accounts, and set the coordinates.

I didn't suspect a crate would fit through the border hole. However, according to BLE, it was only a ten kilometer walk across the neutral zone to a border checkpoint of the O.A.R., the Old American Republic.

It was common knowledge that the O.A.R. accepted defectors from the American Political Union, honoring the two nations' shared history. More importantly, the O.A.R. appreciated the A.P.U.'s strong educational system. With my advanced ability, I anticipated many advantages for myself in the O.A.R.

However, I couldn't foresee as much for BLE.

* * *

Finally, our day of flight came. My plan was so perfect, it was anticlimactic. Our parents never questioned our lie that we were visiting one another. My ingenuity with the crates' innards worked flawlessly. So, I spent most of our transit reading an old novel written before the Second American Civil War.

When we arrived at the gap, we stepped out of our crates into the open sun. We slid right through the border gap.

The hike across the neutral zone was magnificent. Having seen drone videos of A.P.U. Protected Forests hadn't prepared me for the experience of physically walking through nature.

I felt lightheaded upon approaching the Old American Republic border checkpoint. An armed man led us to a waiting area. Quaint paper FAQs indicated that our petitions for defection would be reviewed upon testing and evaluation.

Another man escorted me to a room where I received a multi-subject written exam. The proctor observed me carefully and took notes. Perhaps he was wary of cheaters. But I didn't need to cheat. I crushed the test despite the proctor's irritating stare. Clearly, the O.A.R. badly needed bright people like me!

I paced alone for what seemed like hours. For the first time, my triumph wouldn't remain secret. Soon, I'd have the opportunity to pursue the great life I deserved.

Then, a smiley gentleman entered. From his uniform, I presumed he was important.

"Ma'am, I'm Dan Brendan, O.A.R. Immigration Agent. You'll be pleased with the results of your exam."

I recognized his accent, relaxed and slow, but had never heard it from a live individual. Nevertheless, I savored the praise, eager for more.

"Congratulations JNA-9468," continued Brendan as my anticipation swelled. "Your O.A.R. citizenship application has been hereby granted. Welcome to the land of the free."

I eagerly anticipated my future success in a world where people could be openly compared!

He resumed, "Your being so smart, I reckon you'll want to attend one of our universities. But first we need to discuss your categorization results. You'll belong to Category D, I'm afraid."

That didn't sound too awful. "So...?"

"At school, you'll reside in a Category D living group. If your high achievement continues, you'll have opportunities to work at numerous corporations. But frankly, there'll be limits to what positions you're eligible to hold, what neighborhoods you can live in, who you can marry, and numerous other things."

"I don't understand. Is this because I wasn't born here?"

"That often affects the decision, but not here. Look, our great Old American Republic has four levels: A, B, C, and D."

"And D is the *lowest*? What was my test score? I killed it!"

"The fact you've been admitted here means you did sufficiently well... given your, umm, circumstances."

"What circumstances?"

"You don't know, do you? You and your ridiculous crates. No one's ever told you, have they?"

My stomach fluttered and gurgled. "What?"

"Ma'am, here in the Old American Republic, you're... well... ugly as a dog!" He laughed. "And quite overweight."

"Do you know how *offensive* that is?!"

I couldn't believe my ears. His language went far beyond anything I'd ever heard. In the A.P.U., he'd have suffered more than reeducation videos! In fact, I'm fairly certain he could've been incarcerated under the Correct Speech Act of 2071.

But this wasn't the A.P.U.; it was the O.A.R.

"You seem irate. But expect others to put it less gently."

I was almost missing my crate. BLE and I quickly needed a change of plans!

"Where's my friend BLE? We need to talk."

"BLE-2384? Her new name's 'Bella.' Her exam just missed the margin, but we gave her an extra bump. She's Category B and headed to her new residence."

"What? How did she—"

"You have no sense of reference, do you? Bella's hot! A piece of ass!"

I'd never heard the expression "piece of ass." I let it go.

"If she's so wonderful, why isn't she Category A?"

"Category A? That's for men only! But don't worry about Bella, that sweet thing'll become a pharmaceutical sales rep or news commentator... or anywhere we need a woman in the meeting room to gawk at. Heck, maybe she'll be your boss one day."

I couldn't imagine what vile mode of thinking created a place like this. I was able to run circles around BLE.

Gravely regretting having fled the A.P.U., I was stuck and needed to adjust. Borrowing from *JNA-9468*, I became Janet Niner.

To my delight, several colleges accepted me. Though the odds were stacked against me, I had choices. I traveled across beautiful country to the university I'd selected. My advanced level allowed me to enroll as a sophomore. The Category D living arrangements were cramped, but not as bad as I'd feared.

My roommate Alex was awesome. Her mother had taught her to retain a positive attitude in tough circumstances. I'd known that the A.P.U. had a diverse population, but since everyone hid in crates, it felt entirely theoretical. Although I'd been taught the importance of racial equality, Alex was the first person of African heritage I'd met in person. The more I got to know her, the more I appreciated being free of my crate.

Langer and Jason lived across the hall. According to Alex, they were lovers.

Regretfully, my first glance at Langer was sideways with my brows lowered and nose raised. He must have seen similar looks often, as homosexuality in the O.A.R. had an awful stigma.

I, however, had grown up in the A.P.U., where sexual

orientation was like eye color, all shades thoroughly normal. I was the one perfectly comfortable with it!

There were entirely other reasons, I admit shamefully, for not taking well at first to Langer. Since arriving in the O.A.R., having seen multitudes of live people, I'd begun building comparative yardsticks and found myself brazenly judging others as human instincts dictated.

Langer was tall, but skin and bones. His top jaw jutted forward hideously. His unpleasant face and lack of muscle tone made me uneasy. My glance of disgust must have caused hurt.

His roommate Jason was comically tiny next to Langer. At first, I couldn't take seriously anything puny Jason had to say.

I recognized that my prejudices clashed with my upbringing. But now surrounded by real people, nature was taking over.

Two weeks into school, I'd gotten used to the nasty looks from the Category B's and C's. The university's few A's lived in a Greek-lettered fraternity house. All of them were tall, sturdy, handsome men from select European heritage.

Being a D was tough. We were freely mocked and rarely shown any respect. Every day, someone demeaned me in some manner.

Near the end of my first semester, Langer was in a tough scrape. Another student, a C to my best guess, was punching him around. I assumed this "miscreant" disliked Langer for his sexual orientation. Regardless, Langer was on the ground about to be pummeled. A crowd had gathered to watch.

I don't know what made me do this, but I couldn't let him beat on my fellow D. I leapt out of the crowd and shoved Miscreant with the power of spontaneous rage. He stumbled two meters and tumbled to the ground.

I suddenly realized that I'd been a fool with a death wish for having done that. So, I disappeared among the onlookers before Miscreant could stand up. He never saw me. The crowd could have given me up, my being a D. Fortunately, they didn't seem to care.

Langer successfully escaped. However, my luck appeared to evaporate when a man in a military uniform intercepted me as I fled. He grabbed my arm, though not forcefully. I was terrified of the punishment I'd receive for violence committed against a person of higher category level.

"Janet Niner," he said.

"Please forgive me," I begged contritely, having no idea how he knew my name.

"Are you Janet Niner?"

"Yes sir."

"Someone important needs to speak with you... And your apology baffles me."

Apparently, he was ignorant of my attack upon Miscreant and couldn't have cared less.

* * *

An hour later, I sat in an office in a building reserved for deans and faculty. The man across the desk from me wore a military uniform suggesting significant seniority. In addition to his decorations and rank insignia, he sported a gold pin with the Greek letters of the category A fraternity.

"Please address me as Colonel Hayden," he said. "And frankly, Janet, we need your help."

"*My* help?"

"Everything I'm about to tell you is confidential and

need-to-know. More to the point, if you violate this confidentiality, you'll wind up in a casket."

He had a direct way of speaking. I pondered my chances of surviving the day should I have refused to help him.

He continued, "I understand you have personal experience with crates."

"I'm from the A.P.U.; everyone uses crates."

"No. Specific expertise in electromechanical tampering and code manipulation."

Wondering how he knew that, I imagined lying pointless. I replied with a stutter, "Yes sir... Colonel Hayden."

"I also understand you're one of the more gifted students in the Electrical Engineering Department."

When I'd lived in the A.P.U., I'd ached to hear that type of praise. But after all I'd been through, the comment made me barely crack a smile.

Hayden continued, "We've acquired some crates and require your help. We need you to reprogram them to deliver packages to several highly secure and sensitive geographic coordinates in the A.P.U. You'll need to evade all security protocols designed to protect those locations."

The challenge sounded close to impossible, but I was confident I could ultimately succeed with enough time and additional intelligence regarding the electronic border fence. However, I didn't like the sound of it. It smelled of assassination or terrorism.

"What type of packages?"

Hayden sighed. "Nonlethal electromagnetic impulse weapons designed to disable heavily shielded electronics."

"What are the targets?"

He sighed again. "You have a lot of questions, don't you? It's need-to-know."

"To reprogram the crates, won't I need to know?"

"Are you committing to helping us?"

I lowered my head. I had no idea what I was getting into or what consequences my actions would bring.

"If you demonstrate your patriotism by helping us," Hayden said in a discreet and softer tone, "I can elevate your category level to C. Perhaps even B."

At that moment I should have felt elated. It was the opportunity for things to finally go my way. I was being recognized for my intellectual skills, and my efforts would elevate my social rank. These were the very things I'd hungered for from the beginning when I'd defected from the A.P.U. with BLE. I should have leapt out of my seat and thanked him!

But instead, I sat still, unable to look him in the eye. After all I'd been through, his offer didn't feel comfortable.

"And to answer your question," Hayden said, "the targets are the information systems governing the A.P.U.'s Right-Not-to-Be-Seen database and algorithms. Taken down, two hundred million crates will have no information or restrictions regarding 'live' contacts. We've estimated it'll take several months to piece the system back together, and within that time, more people in the A.P.U. will have seen one another in person than over the past fifty years. Certainly, you understand the significance."

He was aiming to establish liberty for the people of the A.P.U., the liberty I'd so badly sought. But I imagined how it might upset the fragile balance of the two nations' Cold War. Also, I wondered if it might cause many others from the A.P.U. to suffer the indignities that I'd now become so familiar with.

"Swiftly after," Hayden said, "will come Phase 2. Additional crates with EMP weapons will disable vast sections of the electronic fence keeping the A.P.U.'s citizens prisoner. They'll be free to defect here should they choose."

It was plainly clear to me that if I joined Hayden, I would have helped proliferate the O.A.R.'s abominable system of categorizing people, a system that had caused me so much pain.

Looking at the door, I murmured, "I don't know if I can do it."

"Janet," he said, lowering his head slightly, pointing his eyes straight at me. "Janet, please."

"I need to think about it. Can I have time to think about it?"

After a period of silence, he leaned back in his seat.

"I'll give you one week. And we'll be watching you carefully and monitoring your communications. Remember what I said about confidentiality. My assistant will tell you how to get in touch with me. One week, Janet. One week."

* * *

Days later, my friend Francisca walked with me in the rain. She was explaining to me that her family, unlike BLE and I, had entered the O.A.R. through a border that rarely accepted immigrants. She'd been young at the time but believed her father had acquiesced to sexual favors with male border security forces to get his family across the otherwise impenetrable border wall.

I was wrapped up in her story but suspicious that I was being followed. I wasn't certain who was watching me. Was it one of the Category A fraternity brothers trailing me? Or was it the older man with the long hair and beard keeping pace to my right?

Suddenly, one of the Category A's from behind me lunged forward and shoved me with his hip. I tumbled onto a soaked, muddy area of the lawn. Quickly, he had his hands on me. I was terrified.

But he only wanted to roll me around in the mud. His friends laughed and cracked jokes, comparing me to a swine enjoying its own feces. Passersby paused to relish my humiliation.

The man with the long hair and beard stopped in his tracks and made brief eye contact with me. I presumed he was the tail Hayden had put on me. Unfortunately, he did nothing but watch.

Finally, the boys left me alone. Francisca pulled me out of the muck and walked me to my dorm. I'm glad I had her there, but I needed my roommate Alex. I knew she'd find a way to make me feel better.

Was I truly supposed to help these awful people with an act of O.A.R. patriotism? How could I possibly agree to help Hayden knowing that my actions could cause many others to suffer the reprehensible humiliation that I'd experienced in Category D?

At the same time, I couldn't tolerate living like this. My desire to elevate my own category couldn't have burned stronger. It was quite impossible for me to forget Hayden's offer to promote my category level in exchange for my assistance.

I tried to clear my head with a long, hot shower. Disparate thoughts ran through my mind. I was steaming with anger toward Category A and their unchallenged entitlement to do as they pleased.

Yet, I think what stung most about the incident was that the fraternity boy was so damn gorgeous! He was lean and tall. His jaw and cheekbones were solid. His eyes were dark. His full and vibrant head of hair was magnificent. I'd wanted to forgive him immediately. I grasped why the men of Category A were considered our future leaders.

But I stopped myself from waltzing down that path of thought. Soon enough, I felt self-reproach for the ease with which I'd forgiven him.

Once I was clean and dressed, I was finally able to focus upon hope. Clearly, I was in a bad situation, but I was an intelligent individual with the ability to change that.

It was imperative that I contact Hayden. In doing what he'd asked, I'd be appreciated and rewarded for applying my talents. After all, that was the very reason I'd abandoned the A.P.U. and came to the in O.A.R. in the first place! The unfortunate answer to my problem seemed obvious.

I walked out of my dorm room looking my best. I was prepared to accept Hayden's offer and practically felt elevated to Category C already.

Then, Langer stopped me in the hall. He was tearing up. "Janet," he cried my name.

I placed my hand on his arm to comfort him, and he hugged me gently.

"Thank you," he whispered. "I would've gotten clobbered."

It hadn't connected until he'd said that. I'd somehow forgotten how I'd saved Langer from Miscreant. I rubbed my hand against his back and suspected then and there that we'd be good friends for a long time.

Inside though, I heaved in fear of my own potential actions. I'd been about to betray him and Alex and all of my friends in Category D by helping Colonel Hayden and the O.A.R. proliferate its appalling system of social strata.

In that special moment with Langer, I knew I couldn't accept Hayden's offer. If anything, Category D needed to fight back.

* * *

My one week to consider Hayden's offer was expiring. I hoped never to see him again so that I wouldn't have to face the awful decision he'd placed in front me.

I'd grown more depressed, wondering how my life would've unfolded had I stayed in the American Political Union. In my crate, no one could judge me, not by my gender, not by my face, and not by my body. I chastised myself daily for foolishly handing myself a miserable life.

I also considered the more painful prospect that I had no good options regardless of which nation I called home. Perhaps it was my destiny never to receive a fair chance at the life I deserved.

Prof. Houston, on the other hand, represented a unique ray of hope. He cared about all of his students regardless of category. Amazingly, I'd heard he himself was Category A.

I found his kindness and handsome looks a pleasing combination. And he was young for a professor, practically right out of graduate school.

One day during office hours, Prof. Houston was assisting me with a bonus challenge assignment. "Janet, can I ask you your category?" he inquired out of context.

I wanted to tell him. I wanted to explain the injustices I'd witnessed and experienced in the hopes that he'd understand. But at the same time, I was ashamed of my category level and didn't want him to know. Thoroughly conflicted, I couldn't get the words out.

"No need to answer," he continued. "I despise our caste system."

His noble viewpoint surprised me. Whereas I had every reason to hate our abominable system of categories, Prof. Houston, as an A, was endowed with all he needed to prosper.

I remained quiet. I remembered that Hayden might somehow be monitoring the conversation. And paranoia learned from years of A.P.U. communication-policing kept me from speaking my mind. It was difficult remembering that in the O.A.R., there were, in fact, no speech laws inhibiting free expression of one's opinion. We were free to complain about our lower status, yet most simply accepted it as the way life was meant to be.

After leaving the professor's office and upon exiting the building, I saw Hayden rapidly approaching. I considered walking the other way but knew it a lost cause. So, I stopped.

"I need an answer," he said firmly.

I didn't know how to reply. On one hand, there were strong reasons to refuse him. How could I let any more people, those now safely within the borders of the American Political Union, suffer from the O.A.R.'s system of categories? Would my friends in Category D ever forgive me?

Then, I remembered that there was nothing so great about living in an A.P.U. crate and having few real friends at all. And in accepting Hayden's offer, I could be promoted to Category B or C! Furthermore, I was afraid of Hayden and of what might become of me by failing to oblige him.

"I'll help you," I blurted, wishing that my motives were noble.

"Thank you, Janet. Your patriotism has been noted."

My apprehensions, however, didn't fade, as now I had the consequences of my actions to fear.

* * *

I traveled several hundred kilometers to a location near the Old American Republic's capital city. Hayden dealt with the university so that it would accommodate my spending the second semester on an "off-campus assignment."

I joined a team of twelve engineers coding crates. We only needed to re-task thirteen crates, but twenty in total were available to us.

"What are the extra seven crates for?" I asked Grace, our team leader.

"No idea," she answered. "Maybe in case we botch a few."

Working with Grace was an honor. She was immensely sharper than I could ever have hoped to be. And of course, it was unusual for a woman to lead a technical team, especially one who wasn't a ravishing beauty.

It also occurred to me that women made up half the team. I was rather astonished that they'd have allowed such a team to exist. Perhaps Hayden was full of surprises!

* * *

One afternoon several weeks in, the "secretary," as most referred to the administrative assistant, informed me that I had a visitor. I paused and followed.

She led me to a conference room where, to my surprise, BLE was waiting. Considering the circumstances with which we'd last departed, I didn't know whether to hug her or scream at her.

BLE made the decision by hugging me. The fact is, I missed her. She was a piece of my old life I wanted back.

We caught up. BLE, now Bella, attended school in the capital city and got involved with weird political groups. Embarrassed of my D-category, I hid many details of my experiences.

I suspected that I had BLE/Bella to thank in some way. She was the only one with knowledge of my technical skills with crates, and here she was. I probed her on the subject, but she was coy about it. I suspected some link between Hayden and Bella, but I couldn't put my finger on it.

* * *

The date of our EMP-weaponized crate attack on the A.P.U. was approaching. Thanks to a dedicated team, we were near ready. Somehow, I'd become so immersed in the technical challenge that I'd managed to bury my ethical qualms with the project.

Then I received another visitor, Prof. Houston. For my meeting with him, they provided a swanky conference room.

"I suppose you're wondering why I'm here," he said.

I took the comment as rhetorical and didn't respond. Yet, I wanted so much to stop being so quiet in his presence!

"The crate attack needs to be delayed," he continued.

Taken by surprise, I broke out of my bashfulness and hollered, "What? We'll be ready to go!" I didn't want the team's efforts to meet the timeline to go in vain. Also, in the back of my mind, I was restless to complete this and rise out of Category D.

"Isn't that Hayden's call?" I asked in an attempt to dismiss his logic. The professor's role in this was a mystery.

"Hayden and I are colleagues in a sense. The Colonel recruited you because Bella came forward about your crate skills at an AB-Positive meeting. I confirmed your... extraordinary talent... and tenacious spirit and—"

"AB-Positive?" I asked as his kind words made me blush.

"A political organization of Category A's and B's seeking equality reform. Our underground element intensely opposes this one-sided destructive act planned for the A.P.U."

"That doesn't make any sense! *If you wanted to stop the attack, why bring me here in the first place?*"

"Janet, you know these crates better than anyone. We need you to fabricate a technical problem that will delay the attack. Hayden will appear furious, all along knowing what you'll really be up to."

"Which is?"

"Reprogramming the last seven crates. The additional targets must be within our own country, not the A.P.U. When the attack commences and the A.P.U.'s electronic border fence goes down, so will our own border fence. People will be able to transit as they please.

"Imagine people of the O.A.R. seeing that greater equality is possible and that they don't need to accept the status quo.

"And imagine the people of the A.P.U. given back their voices... their right of open expression.

"We hope that the newfound freedom and cross-fertilization between the two nations will breed greater unity and a climate that can truly sustain human progress."

* * *

Ten years have passed since our simultaneous attacks on

the American Political Union and Old American Republic. I live with my husband, the noble professor, down the street from where I grew up. It's an easy stroll to Bella's house. Today, the neighborhood has sidewalks, which in summer, are busy with joggers, bicycles, and baby carriages. Crates are now called "cars," and they all have windows.

I haven't seen Langer and Jason since their wedding a few years ago. It's about time I visited them. They still live near the university, a long way across the country. Fortunately, travel has become easier since the reunification of the United States of America. And it's important to keep reminding myself how precious "live" friends can be.

* * *

This story first appeared in the After Dinner Conversation—December 2020 issue.

Discussion Questions

1. Which country would you want to live in, the one with crates (*the American Political Union*) or the one with the ranking system (*the Old American Republic*)? What does it say about the personality of someone based on the community they choose?

2. When the gates opened in both directions, which country do you think had more people leave? Who do you think left from each country? What were the cultural ramifications of the bilateral exodus on each community?

3. Would the narrator have been offended by the community she migrated to (*the O.A.R.*) if she had been attractive? Didn't she change locations so she could be judged against others, or was it for another reason?

4. It seems like the narrator's main frustration was she was being judged for her looks and not her intelligence. However, to some degree, aren't both of these traits (*attractiveness and intelligence*) determined by a combination of genetics and personal effort? How do you know which traits are okay to judge a person by and which are not? Or, are all traits not suitable for judgment?

5. Could you change one of the communities to make it more acceptable while still keeping the fundamental nature of the community? If so, which one is fixable, and what would you change?

* * *

As You Wish
(Children's Story)

Tyler W. Kurt

* * *

Sad Bear and his friends had been living in the pitch black for years. *Absolute* blackness. They had been put in the trunk shortly after their child, George, had gotten a puppy. There's no sense of time in the blackness so they didn't know how long they'd been in there–months, maybe years.

And then, one day, they heard footsteps in the darkness. Clack, clack, clack, clack. The sound grew louder as it approached. Clack, clack, clack, clack. Would it mean a person would finally set them free? Would this be the person to let them out?

The room shifted violently. Fluffy, a stuffed white rabbit with just one eye, landed on top of Sad Bear, a teddy bear. Mr. Giraffe, a stuffed giraffe, fell onto Dolly, a hard-plastic doll with a yellowed dress and loose threads. Dolly also had, down the side of her face, a long red crayon mark in the shape of an A which made her self-conscious. As the trunk jostled the stuffed animals rolled around on each other until they finally landed with a thud.

The top of the trunk opened. After years of living in the dark the bright light temporarily blinded the animals as they looked up. Their eyes slowly adjusted and they saw, towering over them, an eccentrically-dressed elderly woman.

The woman had white hair that looked as if it hadn't been combed in years and a face thick with wrinkles from smiling. She was 75 years old if she was a day, but her clothes were that of a teenager in a time long past. In fact, her blouse and poodle skirt made it look like she was about to go to a 1950's dance. Her shoes, however, were Converse; one red and one white. And when she spoke, she used the words of an elderly woman but said the words in a light, fairy-like voice.

"Why, hello dears," said the woman. "What do we have here?"

The woman pulled Dolly out of the trunk and examined her. "Now aren't you in sad shape. Old dress, torn threads ..." the woman quickly licked her thumb and started rubbing the red crayon mark off Dolly's face "...it looks like somebody was learning their alphabet on you. Well, this will never do."

The woman looked down at the other stuffed animals in the trunk. "A sad lot indeed." She gently set Dolly down outside the trunk and picked up the stuffed Beagle that was jammed between two other animals. As she lifted the Beagle it exposed its missing leg with stuffing hanging out.

"Be careful with my stuffing!" shouted the Beagle.

"I'm being careful," the woman replied.

"You can hear me?!" the Beagle asked, shocked.

The woman held the Beagle up to look him straight in the eye, because she felt it was more respectful to look someone directly in the eye when you spoke to them. "Well, of course I can. Is your leg in the trunk? Should I get it for you?"

"It's not in the trunk, the puppy ripped it off!"

"Well," the woman said, "if I ever meet that puppy I will have to explain to him the proper way to play with children's toys."

The woman gently set the stuffed Beagle on the ground outside the trunk next to Dolly. "At the very least, I can sew that hole of yours closed so you don't lose any more stuffing. You will be a three-legged dog, but that's better than being a dog that's losing its stuffing."

"Excuse me, ma'am," said Sad Bear from the trunk looking up. Sad Bear, you see, was named Sad Bear because he had a frown sewn on his face for a mouth when he was born. This caused him to be sad even when happy things were happening all around him. "Excuse me ma'am," said Sad Bear. "Can you really hear us?"

The woman picked up Sad Bear to look him in the eyes, just as she had done with the stuffed Beagle. "I suppose I can. Hold on, let me get all of you out of the trunk so we can be properly introduced."

The woman gently set Sad Bear down then reached into the trunk and pulled out all the stuffed animals: Mr. Giraffe, Edwina the elephant, as well as Fluffy the white rabbit, Mr. Panda, and a rainbow unicorn that all the other animals made fun of because she stood out and had no name at all. She grabbed them all, and, one by one, lined them all up in a circle, so they could have a proper conversation.

When they were all sitting in their places, Fluffy the stuffed white rabbit, looked up at the woman and spoke first, "Excuse me Miss, but how is it you can hear us?" he said in a rabbit's squeaky voice.

"Well," the woman said, sitting down cross-legged in front of them, a rather impressive feat, considering her age, "you all can hear each other, can't you?"

"Yes," said Fluffy, "but we're stuffed animals and you're a real person. And real people can't hear stuffed animals, except sometimes when they are very young."

"I guess I never grew up," the woman replied. Then she glanced around at the other stuffed animals in the circle to examine them. "Well, you all are a motley group in dire need of repairs, if you don't mind me saying."

"We have been in the trunk a very long time," said Sad Bear. "And before we got put away by George, that was our child, the puppy would play with us very rough." The three-legged Beagle held up his stump where his leg used to be to prove his point. The woman looked over at the Beagle.

"Indeed," replied the woman looking where his leg used to be. "But, like I said, I will fix you. I will fix *all* of you, and you'll be in ship-shape and ready to go to a new home in no time. So, let's make a list of all the things that need to be fixed. First, of course, my Beagle friend, I will sew your leg hole shut so you can stop losing stuffing. Or, if you would prefer, I can make you a new leg that matches."

"You can do that?" asked the Beagle in wonder.

"Why, of course I can," said the woman, who took out a small notepad and a pencil to write notes as she spoke. "One new Beagle leg."

"Excuse me ma'am," Dolly said, seeing her chance. "My dress is very dirty, you see, and it has yellowed with age when it should be white...and the threads are all coming out–"

"–Yes, yes, of course," the woman interrupted. "I shall sew you a new white one." The woman spoke out loud as she wrote in her notepad, "One new white dress. You appear to be a size negative 32, is that correct?"

Dolly blushed and lowered her head. "Why, yes ma'am, that's correct."

"How many dresses would you like?"

"I like?" Dolly asked.

"Yes. How many dresses would you like me to make for you?"

"Well," said Dolly, "I've only ever had the one."

"I'll make you three to get you started, and more later if you want." Dolly heard this and blushed.

Fluffy, the white rabbit, spoke up next in his squeaky rabbit voice. "I lost one of my eyes to the dog; could you sew me on a new eye?"

"Oh my, yes, I see that. That will never do. I will find you a new eye to sew on." The woman wrote in her notepad as she spoke. "One new rabbit eye."

"Actually," Fluffy said, "if it's not too much to ask, my eyesight wasn't all that good even before with two eyes. You see, when I was born my eyes were made with the cheapest plastic. Do you think you could sew on *better* eyes so that I can see better than before?"

"I don't see why not."

"And I..." said Mr. Panda, speaking up for the first time in a Panda's deep proper voice. "I am quite fat, even for a

Panda. Would it be too much trouble for you to take some of my stuffing out? Not all of it, mind you, just a little bit, so that I still look like a Panda, but I look like a *thin* Panda?"

"Of course," said the woman. "What else? I can change anything you want. I can make you taller, or shorter, or fatter, or thinner. I can change your eyes, or even your fur. As a matter of fact, while I'm at it, would anyone else like me to take some of their stuffing out?" The elephant's trunk went up.

Mr. Giraffe, a stuffed orange and brown giraffe that spoke very quickly when he spoke, spoke up next. "I know I'm a giraffe. And I know giraffes have long necks, but I think I look very silly standing next to everyone else with such a long heck. I would like 4 1/4 inches taken off of my neck please."

"Of course," the woman replied with a smile and note in her notebook. "Exactly 4 and 1/4 inches...."

"You can do that?" asked the very shy rainbow unicorn.

"Yes I can."

"Well, then could you..." said the unicorn very softly. "You see, I'm a unicorn–"

"–Yes, I see that," said the woman. "Unicorns are very rare and very special indeed."

"Yes, but you see," said the unicorn almost in a whisper, "I don't want to be rare and special. Could you...please...take off my unicorn horn and make my fur brown, so that people would think I was a horse?"

The woman gave a slow nod-like bow. "If that is what you wish." The only animal that hadn't asked for anything was Sad Bear and so, the woman turned to him last. "And what about you Mr. Bear, that frown stitched on your face looks terribly sad. You must be sad all the time."

"I am," said Sad Bear. "From the first day I was made I've always had this frown on my face, and so I've always been sad."

"Well then, I shall *fix* that too. It won't take but a minute. I shall take that stitching out and stitch a smile on your face, so you will always be happy even when sad things are happening."

"Thank you," responded Sad Bear politely. "But if it's all the same to you, I think I'd like to keep my frown."

"Well, why would you want to do that? I am going to fix his leg, and her dress, and give him two brand new eyes that are better than the cheap plastic eyes he was born with. I'm going to turn a unicorn into a horse, take the stuffing out of Mr. Panda and his elephant friend, and make the giraffe's neck shorter. As long as I am doing all of those things, I could just as well sew a smile on your face."

"Yes, I'm sure you could," said Sad Bear. "And thank you for helping all my friends, but you see, ma'am, my name is 'Sad Bear' because I have a frown on my face. Because I *am* a Sad Bear."

"I see, but you don't have to be sad," said the woman. "Don't you know that being *happy* is good and being *sad* is bad. Just like missing a leg is bad and having all your legs is good. And having one eye is bad, and having two eyes is good, and having two very good eyes is even better still. And why would you want to be a unicorn or a giraffe and stand out, when you can be so very average and blend in? Don't you want to be fixed?"

Sad Bear thought about this for a while and thought a long time about how best to explain himself without offending the eccentrically dressed woman or his friends.

"I think..." said Sad Bear slowly, "...even though I have a

frown sewn on my face, and I am sad, even when good things are happening... I think..." said Sad Bear, "...I would prefer to just be me. Even if, you see, that is just a sad bear."

"I see," said the woman with a warm smile and a nod. "As you wish."

* * *

This story first appeared in the After Dinner Conversation—October 2020 issue.

Discussion Questions

1. Which of the toys asked for things that you think were okay for them to ask for? As a reminder, the beagle wanted his torn off leg sewn back on, the doll wanted a new dress, the panda and elephant wanted to have some stuffing removed. The unicorn wanted to look like a horse, and the rabbit wanted his eyes replaced with better eyes. What is the distinction between each request being a "good request," and a "bad request?"

2. What are the things about us that we should improve, or correct, and what are the things we should leave alone? What is the distinction between the two?

3. Was Sad Bear right in refusing the woman's offer to remove his frown and sew a smile on his face so he would always be happy? Why/why not?

4. If someone could magically fix something about you, or improve something to make you better, would you let them? What would you change?

5. How do you know when is it better to try and fix the things you are self-conscious about, versus learn to embrace and love them?

* * *

Author Information

A Wolf on The Bus

Matthew Wallace currently lives in Houston, Texas with his incredible wife, daughter, and pug named Captain Oats. In addition to being a published short fiction author, and an aspiring novelist, he has performed stand-up comedy across the United States of America. He believes change is possible.

Teddy And Roosevelt

Steven Simoncic's work has appeared in *CRAFT*, *Arts and Letters*, *Conclave*, *Ampersand*, *Fractured Literary*, *Beyond Words*, and *Ariel Publishing* among others. He has been nominated for a Pushcart Prize, was a finalist for the Susan Atefat Fiction Prize, and was included in the *Best American Essays 2016*. As a playwright, Steven has had productions in Chicago, LA, NY and London. He was a semi-finalist at the Eugene O'Neill National Playwright Conference and a finalist for the Woodward/Newman Drama Award. Steven holds a BBA from the University of Michigan, an MFA from Warren Wilson, and an MLA from the University of Chicago.

The Hanging Man

Margery Topper Weinstein is an editor and writer based in New York City. In addition to short stories, Margery writes nonfiction pieces on healthcare, work life and travel. She loves psychological thriller stories, including those full of dark humor. X (Twitter) *@MargeryW*; Instagram *@margerytweinstein*; LinkedIn *@margery-weinstein-86a65035*

Never Enough (Until You Earn It)

Dr. Raymond is a Family and Emergency Physician. He practiced in eight countries in four languages and is currently living in Austria with his wife. When not volunteering his practice skills, he is writing, lecturing, or scuba diving. He has multiple medical citations, and is published in *Flash Fiction Magazine*, *LITRO*, *The Examined Life Journal*, *The Satirist*, *Chicago Literati*, and many others. He is the fiction editor of *SavagePlanets* magazine. *www.savageplanets.com*

Drag Brunch

Mark Bessen (he/him) is a queer writer based in Austin, Texas, originally from Southern California. He holds a BA in English from Stanford, and his fiction and essays have been featured in *Epiphany*, *The Offing*, *Taco Bell Quarterly*, *New South*, *Tahoma Literary Review*, and elsewhere. Twitter *@MarkBessen*

What We Talk About When We Talk About Reincarnation

Edward Daschle (he/him/his) is a student of fiction in the University of Maryland's creative writing MFA program. He grew up in the Pacific Northwest, land of serial killers and Sasquatch, deadly mountains and overcast skies. His fiction also appears in *Grim & Gilded*, *Stoneboat Literary Journal*, *Defunct*, and *OFIC Magazine*.

The Draft

Jan McCleery spent her career as a software engineer start-up founder, and applies her independent woman experiences in a man's world to her writing and thought processes. Jan became a California Delta activist and formed a nonprofit to fight the "water wars." Jan has also published nine books, including her recent spy novel series. *www.FromTheDuckPond.com*

The Human Experience

Jared Cappel's prose has appeared or is set to appear in various publications including *Idle Ink*, *Literally Stories*, and *City. River. Tree.* When he's not writing, he enjoys creating digital art known for its abstract imagery and vibrant use of color. A lover of wordplay, he's ranked as one of the top 50 Scrabble players in North America. *fineartamerica.com/profiles/jared-cappel*

The Crate

David Rich lives with his wife and two daughters in the Boston area. His short fiction has appeared in *Bards & Sages Quarterly*, *Bewildering Stories*, *Youth Imagination*, and *The Macabre Museum*. David works in the biotech industry. He holds a Bachelor's and PhD from the MIT in engineering fields.

As You Wish

Tyler W. Kurt self-identifies as a teacher, writer, traveler, and trail runner. He left the practice of law to spend five years teaching Socratic discussion classes in a charter school. He has visited 55+ countries and lived in Mozambique, China, Thailand, and Argentina. Accordingly, he has learned and forgotten Portuguese, Chinese, and Spanish.

Additional Information

Reviews

If you enjoyed reading these stories, please consider doing an online review. It's only a few seconds of your time, but it is very important in continuing the series. Good reviews mean higher rankings. Higher rankings mean more sales and a greater ability to release stories.

Print Books

https://www.afterdinnerconversation.com

Purchase our growing collection of print anthologies, "Best of," and themed print book collections. Available from our website, online bookstores, and by order from your local bookstore.

Podcast Discussions/Audiobooks

https://www.afterdinnerconversation.com/podcastlinks

Listen to our podcast discussions and audiobooks of After Dinner Conversation short stories on Apple, Spotify, or wherever podcasts are played. Or, if you prefer, watch the podcasts on our YouTube channel or download the .mp3 file directly from our website.

Patreon

https://www.patreon.com/afterdinnerconversation

Get early access to short stories and ad-free podcasts. New supporters also get a free digital copy of the anthology *After Dinner Conversation–Season One*. Support us on Patreon!

Book Clubs/Classrooms

https://www.afterdinnerconversation.com/book-club-downloads

After Dinner Conversation supports book clubs! Receive free short stories for your book club to read and discuss!

Social

Connect with us on Facebook, YouTube, Instagram, TikTok, Substack, and Twitter.